To Luke, Good &
Matty
Saint
Happy New Year

10/01/18

Anonymous
in a
town that talks 2

CON O'DONNELL

authorHOUSE®

AuthorHouse™ UK
1663 Liberty Drive
Bloomington, IN 47403 USA
www.authorhouse.co.uk
Phone: 0800.197.4150

Published by AuthorHouse 12/22/2017

ISBN: 978-1-5462-8635-6 (sc)
ISBN: 978-1-5462-8634-9 (e)

Blowjobs Holiday In The Sun Miss Sixty Shoes

What sort of job do you need,
to pay for those shoes,
Whatever, you need a holiday,
to get rid of all those blues,
your tongue must be numb,
after all those blows,
you need miss sixty shoes,
to go with those clothes,
sketchers are cool,
blowjobs are better,
even tastier they are,
without a French letter!!!

10/1

That time already?
5/1 now!
They're falling steady,
but bouncing back up,
I'm not known,
where to stand?
lookout below,
here comes the band.

14 Lines

As I sat on it,
I thought of a sonnet,
but the jobs not over,
til the paper works done,
when I flush away the waste,
my pen and paper will be at one,
to scroll the scribe,
from the calligraphy tribe,
I'll write the words,
from the inscriptions that hide,
I hope it's free access,
because I've no money for a bribe!
Ah! Now I remember the nubile young girl at the gate,
maybe she'll let me in if I take her out for a date.

35 Days And 35 Nights

35 days and 35 nights,
the company's good,
but the food gives you the shites!
No shelter for cover,
only this hospitall,
but it's nice to get care,
from the staff down the hall,
It must be a requirement,
to be a bloody beauty,
cause they're all very pretty,
and that's just the men!
The nurses look gorgeous,
so I'll say it again,
their eyes and their hair,
not to mention their care,
there's only one thing,
but I'll let it be,
you have to make your own fucking tea!!!
But the service is good,
cos a guy I only met,
just gave me some food,
so it's a good place to visit,
is that understood!!!

0352 Hrs.....Bedtime

Archimedes said.... "give me a fulcrum large enough, a
lever long enough,
and a place to stand....and I will move the world."
When I read these words,
in my mind it provoked thoughts,
sent shivers down my spine,
and sent a chill to my toes that curled.
So all I ask is a pen that's mightier than the sword,
And I will write the speak of the written word.
It may invoke thought,
and send a rumble through your brain,
but it's not impossible to think so hard that you'll go insane!
So listen to every word of what people say,
It may improve your life and help you out some day.

Reasons:
I was after being told to go to bed by Sarah like a
good little boy cos it was past my bedtime. And that
she doesn't make the law, she just enforces it. (I was
25) She means well but there's room for common
sense in every walk of life! (written on original)

A Kiss

Tender and gentle,
so simple a thing,
amazing the pleasure,
a kiss can bring,
provoking thoughts,
that last the day,
be careful not,
to think that way,
for deep thinking,
even when necessary,
takes away a kisses simplicity,
and simplicity is what makes it sweet,
so let it lie,
and let things be,
tomorrow a kiss,
may come again,
don't fret and worry,
if and when.

A Kiss

What's in a question?
All the time.
Why's always there,
in the meaning of rhyme,
itch the scratch,
and scratch the itch,
is a kiss a kiss,
without a hitch,
some can't differentiate,
for them life's a bitch,
the grey area's blue,
and it makes them see red,
black at night,
but sometimes white instead,
yet for those that know,
it's simple and sweet,
it's lips and minds,
just happening to meet.
A thought
I thought I saw a thought,
but it went quickly and I forgot.
It came again but did not refrain,
its times its own within this spherical dome,
bouncing around perpetual thoughts,

no time to wait in parking lots,
there's tracks and traces and empty places,
forks and junctions and roundabouts,
all roads taken without any doubts,
all points of the compass,
all are combined,
for that any one instant,
in anyone's mind.

Sit And Spin! Ages 6 To 9

AA

The aunt @ the back,
said anxiety attack,
poor uncle Neil,
I know how you feel,
Cos we've got one, two,
peas in a pod,
twins from hell,
or sometimes god,
bad enough on their own,
but with their forces combined,
it's impossible to unwind,
you gotta close your ears,
as they talk at each other,
it is a scene that would raise a smile,
on a man who is blind.
In vino veritas,
as they spill their news,
and the rest of us look on,
and sing the blues.
My favourite model auntie,
dressed to the nines with style,

at christmas and birthdays,
she arrives with presents by the pile,
for an uncle and aunt
you couldn't meet better,
they're straight to the point,
just like a red setter,
so till I see them,
they'll Carpe Diem!

Abounds

My mind abounds,
on the grounds,
of a vivid and a wild imagination,
from a one man army,
loose cannon,
lone gun!
To the charmer of millions,
but the lover of one,
far-fetched dreams,
if aired for discussion,
but I made pipes to keep them in,
so tell me,
who holds the key?

Ac Milan And Time

It's early in the game,
so who can tell,
but inzaghi's on the ball,
about to unleash hell,
there's a rumble in the crowd,
see the roar in their throats swell,
it's time to let go,
top corner style,
the keeper reaches to save,
but misses by a mile,
it's AC Milan time,
time for AC Milan,
and with Gareth as the engine,
the midfield Irish man,
so if anyone will take them,
straight to the top,
Gareth'll do it,
without any stop.

Alien Nation

A terrorist state to be in,
fear across the nation,
it's the deliberation of this deleterious deliquent,
that causes the frustration,
it's their need to understand,
why not let me be?
Leave me alone I'm grand,
so fuck you all,
get me or don't,
I'll lose no life nor sleep,
if you do or won't.

Animals

Neanderthal to homo-sapien,
Darwin's theory seems to fit,
the evidence is there,
where the first fire was lit,
Gavin said to me,
of all the people he'd like to meet,
was the guy who stole the flame,
from underneath the great Gods feet,
Evolution started somewhere,
but as animals some think it's was us,
what about the mammals and birds and fish,
it's the superior attitude that's causing all the fuss,
global warming and extinction,
both go hand and hand,
the ivory tusks in South Arica,
for less than a couple of Rand,
Leopard skin rugs,
polar bear coats,
only the Eskimos have those rights,
and those indigenous to natures land,
who have the foresight,
they don't kill the young,
before they procreate,
only the homo-sapiens whites do that,

and use another as bait,
two birds with one stone,
Is not how they should see,
It's pretty obvious to me,
Is it obvious to ye?

Armageddon

Is it real?
We see but we do not feel,
apathy reigns all sympathy to heel.
If you do the right thing,
you're brought to your knees,
and punishment delivered in various degrees.
Hunger, pollution,
and the superpowers resistance,
threatens the lifespan,
of our entire existence.
It's a catharsis of dreams,
of people in power,
planted centuries ago,
it's now a withering flower.
The chaotic energy,
of the manmade compression,
the molecular level agitated,
without discretion,
as the compression continues,
the agitation increases,
the friction finds friendships,
falling to pieces,

so unless the voice of the people,
don't sing the same rhyme,
the gate won't stop,
the next big bang in time.

Autumn

Spring forward
fall back,
the cycle of life,
is on its perpetual track,
to sleep the sleep,
of a thousand years,
and wake when winters,
thawed from our fears,
the fall of a leaf,
spreading seed where it lands,
the Glory of life,
is in your God given hand.

Axe No Questions. Tell No Lies

The politics of power,
has always caught my eye,
from the schoolyard as a kid,
to watching grown men lie.
The moment it was defined for me,
what politics really was,
the belief in a change for the better,
caused a stirring in my clause.
The purple shroud of mystery,
that's worn with so much pride,
is just a scam to block the dam,
so every lamb can hide.
Out in the open,
where we all can see,
is where I stand upon the tree,
branches supporting,
to the roots in the ground,
how long will they stand there,
When the axe is found?
Chipping away with every mistake,
I'll whip up the wind that'll make the bow break.
It's the safety net then,
that's formed through opinion,

deciding if their fate,
feels like a minion.
Correctness or not,
conversations are forgotten,
but insults intended,
fester until they're rotten.

Back to reality?

So what's next
After this game?
Is it back to normal
or more of the same?
No drugs or eaves dropping,
or peering eyes,
I can be myself,
no need for lock and key.
I can show my brilliance,
leave it all in the past,
as a distant memory,
forget myself a little,
if only a little at a time,
there are boundries,
like a pitch with lime,
stay within the realm of society,
but bollicks to that!
It just ain't me!
I'll be myself,
without the added hi
but I'm still gonna soar,
I'll still rise and fly,
Phoenix from the flames,
inside your reality,

Don't try and rationalize,
or put me in a box,
I'm the odd one out,
in 10 million pairs of socks!!!

Believe

Do you believe?
Cos I believe it's true,
but what's the question I'm telling you?
It's a rhetoric retort,
of an age old conundrum,
an answer of sort,
to believe in yourself,
I believe in me,
watch this space,
see me blast into orbit,
and at last I'll be free,
the true colours will shine,
and they'll all be mine,
I'll use it for good,
to help my friends and family,
they may not know where they stand now,
but they know where they stood,
I take them at face value,
cos I love and trust them all,
they stand up for what they believe,
they stand proud and tall,
they'll begin to believe when they see the real me,
my capabilities and acumen,
will astound and amaze,

hidden talents I secreted,
away from the worlds view,
so give them 3D glasses,
and let them GAZE!

Bending The Rules

Well fuck me pink,
we're not fucking kids,
what the hell do you think?
I'll have to grab your heads,
and stick them in the sink.
I'll turn on the hot,
then on with the cold,
what's that you say?
"Get to bed - do as your told",
snowballs chance in hell,
is what I will tell,
I've never done it before,
well not that I'm aware of,
but my parents are masters,
in the art of bluff,
so unbeknownst to me,
it might have occurred,
but for you'all to tell me,
is pretty absurd,
it stretches my patience,
beyond new realms like a catapult,
we're not fucking children,
I'm a fully grown adult!!
So don't patronize or chastize,

or look at me with those eyes,
or talk with a sympathetic voice,
If you bend a few rules,
then we can all rejoice!!

Biomedical Material

Should it be there,
or should it not?
Definitely without it,
you would be caught!
Just cos you use it,
it doesn't say who you are,
it's not material,
like a Jaguar.
You may need it from birth,
but that can't be helped,
it all began as an embryo,
and now the material you need is necessarily bio,
but it'll keep you from pain,
and hopefully sane,
out of trouble and strife,
and give you a good life!

Bog Roll Blues

Disphoric constipation,
deep within my bowel,
if only I could scrape it out,
with the mathematicians trowel,
the pen may be mightier than the sword,
but the pencil is best of all,
because once prepaired,
it'll write in the sun and even in rainfall,
with friends like you Mr. Vindaloo,
who needs enemas,
just for me findaloo,
colonic irrigation,
that's nutritious too!

Bonnie and Clyde

A writing young spark from Donegal,
was so bright his friends said he knew it all,
but this minx of a woman blew it all.

She was Donegal,
and she too thought she knew it all,
but she met this young stud from Donegal,
who also in her head blew it all.

So they blew it all together,
the proverbial birds of a feather,
they turned to acting,
shoplifting and transacting.

This Bonnie and Clyde from the North West,
won an Oscar! They are the best!

Borderline

All the boundries and lines,
within the confines,
of your apparent liberty,
disinhibited free mind,
who says they knew?
Are they sure it was you?
Ah it's yourself,
how do ye do?
But back to the question,
cos we side stepped and flew,
and if you do it again,
I'll turn the airwaves blue,
and flutter around this compound,
like a coked up cuckoo,
so you knew all along?
But didn't say?
no-one ever asked,
they just let me play,
I was encouraged at home,
but restricted at school,
I didn't like rules,
and enjoyed playing the fool,
so to those who called me a waster,
let this be a little taster,

the tip of the ice berg,
on your tongue,
and I'll write and sing the verse,
of the songs that are yet unsung.

Bread head

Fresh from the head,
like freshly cooked bread,
don't shine too brightly,
or expect something frightfully,
it's happened to me,
all of my life,
my device was to rhyme,
and I do mean strife,
hospital once,
but now it's been twice,
now you've bipolar illness,
and it's not like lice,
you can't have a good wash,
and it'll all be gone,
you must cleanse you soul,
at the stroke of dawn,
a new day to progress and strive,
every time you wake up and take a breath,
it's a good day to be alive.

BUNI-polar

Bipolar or Uni,
or out and out loony,
so I dropped my trousers,
and showed her a moony,
the trousers were mental,
a metaphor so to speak,
and when I said what I said,
threw her fingers she did peak,
her question arose from the book of words mind,
the answer was in there,
but with blinkers on,
people do go blind,
she said you're not Uni-polar,
there's no such thing,
Ah! Ha! said my head,
ding a ling ling,
so I asked her a question,
"there's no Uni but there's Bi?"
Yes she said and I'll tell you why,
but I interrupted,
and told her I only go high,
but she interrupted back,
and said "let me explain" with a frown,
said she you're telling me,

you don't go down?
I said I'd stay down all day,
to which she was affronted,
probably a little turned on,
but embarrassment took over,
cause I'd certainly hit the right buttons,
that definitely drove her,
then insult to injury,
I couldn't let it ly,
cause if you do that,
opportunities pass you by,
so I told her to warn the doc,
it doesn't exist,
and in all his years of reading,
there's something he missed,
this startled her a bit,
or should I say a bit more,
a double whammy in 3 minutes,
is quite a good score,
but I told her not to worry,
and that I would set him straight,
but she insisted they'd confer,
so they both can enjoy the bait!

Bunnies

I've let you undress me,
within your minds eye,
I didn't let you,
It's yours for the taking,
and fantasy making,
but not hearts breaking,
friends forever,
fuck buddies of a kind,
but I need no other,
cause I have you in my mind.

A busy day

A busy day,
but it's home time soon,
hip-hip hooray,
no time to even bless myself,
let alone think,
even when I'm thirsty,
I forget to drink,
but 15 minutes and counting,
I'll be in the pub,
and it'll drink I'm after,
not the grub!
Let's hope tomorrow,
will soon be over,
Because I'm planning on beer,
and a massive hangover,
I'm long on patients,
but they're short on temper,
they like fucking me around,
just for fun,
and it leaves me drinking,
like a dog with distemper,
but busy is good,
it passes the time,
it feels at the end of the day,

you deserve the wine,
but I enjoy the work,
it gives me a thrill,
to mix with Geniuses,
and the mentally ill!!!

By Emma

Not Con by nature,
but only by name,
he's true as they come,
but ain't all that sane,
with his funky wee hat,
that sits on his head,
as he bops along to his 'Eminem'.
He's as fit as they come,
I'm telling you now,
Defo for a fling,
and as for that bum.
So Con by name,
not by nature,
you better watch that bum,
Coz I'm coming to take her!!

Catharsis

We're all as one,
just moving along,
everythings going strong,
what's done is gone,
we look to the future,
remember the nice bits of the past,
they remain in our minds,
and forever last,
then monsoon, typhoon, earthquake
and tidal wave,
hits our happy home,
nearly everyone escaped,
but there's one we cannot save,
he's gone with God now,
hangs out with Joey Dunlop,
and the like,
happily doing donuts,
on his new Ducati bike,
so don't fear his absence,
or reject his presence,
he's just trying to get through,

from him to you,
when it happens again,
relax and take it in,
and the path to healing will slowly begin.

C'est la vie

There's no fault,
there's no blame,
everything is as it was,
it's all the same,
pain follows pleasure,
as night follows day,
it make take a while,
but you'll again say hooray,
drop the guard for a second,
on unfounded trust,
so learn the lesson again,
if you must you must,
the trusts still there,
but in a different way,
c'est melier,
I have to say.

Chair

Bouncing as he learns his first word,
and smiles his first smile,
sitting up high as he learns,
to feed himself this growing child,
tall enough to sit in front,
seatbelt on,
sit up straight,
first day in class,
no comfort here but new friends are great,
waiting for trial,
juvenile thief and mother tense,
"Take a seat",
"Take the weight of your feet",
"Sit there till you get some sense"
We'll make it understandable and concise,
not long till it'll condense,
now sit on your throne,
but listen to advice,
your vocation and rightful place,
after all it costs nothing to be nice.

Children

From infancy to infamy,
kids are born without sin,
so the habits we give them,
always sink in,
be good to your child,
because one day they'll be in your shoes,
and need to retrieve from their memories,
your valid views,
kids are cool,
from the mouths of babes,
caught many a fool,
we thought were Lincoln Abes,
my father always says,
that he personally wears,
his inner child on the outside,
if it bothers some people,
he says who cares?
But my ma always says,
I never grew out of the two's,
but there's a lot of us out there,
don't hide yourself away,
and you will not loose.

Childs play

One flew into the cuckoo next,
looking for guidance,
and a well earned rest.
The resultant reception,
was a rather mixed bag,
most of the cool nurses were there,
but there still remains the odd toe-rag,
rules have been added,
subtracted and doubled,
so it's understandable to see,
why we are all so troubled,
it's like playing football with a friend,
who keeps moving the post,
demoralizing our spirits,
til all you are left with ghosts,
but in the true fighting Irish style,
we show our true Irish form,
rise above all bureaucracy,
and sail through the storm,
we're not the untouchables,
that's why we came here for your help,
and if we step out of line,
you'll give us a skelp,
but a bit of common sense,

should be the prevailing wind,
not a stereotypical view,
that we all have sinned,
this is directed,
at only one or two,
so thanks and God bless to y'all,
I must go back,
to from where I flew.

Chocolate

It's beautiful smooth in texture,
especially when rubbed on your body,
It's crunchie @ first then melts in your mouth,
dairymilks the only one for me,
tomorrow I've got an AA meeting,
shake rattle and roll,
oh for a bar I'd sell my soul,
It's nice to receive on your birthday,
I'd kill for a chocolate bowl,
Santa Claus ya bastard you ate all my sweets,
just as well it's Christmas day and I'm away to mass,
but when I get back I'll get the Easter
bunny to kick your fucking ass,
he'll pull out all your teeth,
and leave them for the fairy,
I'd kill for Sarah's ass,
I'd put it in my pipe and smoke it with some grass,
they scream it's the ring of fire,
throw her on the pire,
but that's not fair cos she's so nice,
so lets rap her up in sugar and spice.

Cigarette butts

The very last drag,
at the end of the fag,
it's the end of one,
and start of another,
can I burn a fag for ye?
said my fellow brother,
I'll leave you my butt,
said the guys mother,
cigarettes are bad for ye,
I've told ye before,
we've all known that,
since the days of yore!
Do as I say,
not as I do,
you'll live a longer life,
when the cigarette butts are few.

Clingy

I apologize not!
For what I'll do,
I'll stick to your mind,
like sniffing super glue,
breathing straight to your brain,
through all barrier of pain,
picking up things,
you never knew,
next thing you're saying it,
straight from the heart,
when it's fabricated lunacy,
with the stench of a fart,
so gather up your minds belongings,
while they're still intact,
start the revolution now,
not after the fact!

Cliona

Red lips,
and hair clips,
and big deep blue eyes,
and wavy mad hair,
with artistic dyes,
that cute sexy laugh,
that so turns me on,
and that puppy dog look,
that says"come to bed Con",
the smell of your scent,
the feel of your touch,
these are just some of the reasons,
why I love you so much.

Closet undone

A problem shared is a problem halved,
so the more people I tell,
the greater the division will be,
so much so it'll be an ever decreasing circle of 10 -n,
the big bang occurred last year,
but now I'm in the refining stages,
there's a bit to go,
but I'm getting there,
with the burden gone,
life moves on,
it tried to drag me down,
and look like a clown,
but I stood up to be counted,
and my white horse I mounted,
I've done the crime,
and I've done my time,
and they're possibly right,
that it doesn't pay,
but fuck it!
Who cares?
Hi ho silver away!!!

Coinyabeta

The pleasures of wanking

It's a solitary game something like patience,
but if you work to hard you'll end up a patient,
it's a fierce boring job but some ones got to do it,
a wanks not for Christmas it's for the rest of your life,
and you'll have to go solo,
till you find a girl or a wife,
wank with your left,
wank with your right,
be ambidextrous,
and let yourself take flight,
for when you get good,
you learn self control,
restraint and delivery,
no matter the toll,
so practice your moves,
let those fingers find their grooves,
like a pianist and his piano,
how funny it is they go together,
if only this feeling could last forever!

Comply

Slow up,
slow down,
round and round,
the cage must open
before I drown,
thoughts slowing,
then racing,
but always faster than yours,
so you'll never understand,
give you a 3rd degree,
and you still won't see,
because you're not me.

i am Leo i am 8 years old i think Con is SHit.

Concert

It's concert day,
hip-hip hooray,
will I get out?
You're fucking right I will,
Whatever it takes,
If it means blood to spill,
but I'd prefer a peaceful exit,
and hasty return,
because the passion inside,
is on the eternal burn.
So I need a release,
don't fence me in,
to do it to me,
would be a terrible sin!
I gotta feel the beat,
the sweating of bodies,
feel the heat!
Stand in the queue,
waiting for my soft drink,
those youngsters drinking beer,
will get sick me does think!!
But listen to the song,
and hear the words,
I've to go to the toilet Ughh!!

Look at those turds!!!
Is there no cleaner,
because there is defo a screener,
he took my stash,
coming in the gate,
but the music's a substitute,
it'll compensate!!!

Concise

My mental state,
I try to encapsulate,
within my poem and song,
can't you read between the lines?
can't anyone see what's going on?
I explain it as concisely as anyone could,
but it falls on deaf ears,
are people's heads like wood?
Would they let me go if like normal I act?
Or give me a little,
then retract?
It's fucking me up,
inside within,
I try to find the words,
but don't know where to begin,
I'll try again,
like one and one is two,
I'll take out my calculator,
even better - an abacus,
but tractatus - logico Philosophicus,
it's selective listening,
they can't see what I feel,

cos only what I let them,
is what they think for real,
well in days or weeks I will be gone,
but you'll be stuck here for your whole life LONG!

Confidence

Does a do don't,
when a will won't,
of course it will,
do does when it won't,
even when it will,
I will!

CONformity

Is this what normal is supposed to be?
Boredom x boredom x 10 to the 6 times 3,
they don't lighten your mood,
they try to extinguish you flare,
because for their closed minds and blind eyes,
it's too much glare,
well frankly my dear people,
I don't fucking care,
Here I am,
take me as I come,
grandiose plans or not,
they'll put me number 1.

Cricket

Serious or not,
inter-club or recreational,
we've got the lot,
a strangers a friend,
you just haven't met,
there's meetings and groups,
4 dimension don't forget.
And after these gatherings,
there's always a time extension,
for intermingling, flesh pressing,
ice breaking the tension,
at the crest of the wave,
progress to another,
new life, new sport,
there's 45 to choose from,
one or the other,
so it's down to you,
cause only you can pick it,
I'd recommend all of them,
especially the cricket,
yeah, it's in the category of sports,
it just gets bad press,
because of the English,
who tied to oppress,

but without aul Lizzy,
the college wouldn't exist,
so for inspirational people,
she's top of the list.

Crosswords

Crosswords can often be a crossroads,
you've to look at the words,
and decide the mode,
your train of thought,
the path to take,
if you think you're right,
and write it in,
and then you're wrong,
well then you're caught!
So I suggest you use a pencil,
and when using a pen,
keep it neat,
so use a stencil!
Cos if you want the money.
They've to be able to read it.
And if there's enough of a prize,
you can visit somewhere sunny,
so before you send it in,
make sure it's right and the words are neat,
then you'll be put in the draw,
with a chance to win.

Crystal clear

Is it four walls,
or an opaque fence,
that frustrates the mind,
and leaves out common sense.
They tell me it's freedom,
but I don't believe'um,
There's fuck all to do,
but go for a beer,
but visitors are comin,
so I must stay here!
Where the hell are they?
What's keeping them?
Stuck in traffic,
stuck in a metal hem,
hemmed in by cars,
and no way out,
I can sympathize with them,
it makes me scream and shout,
so let me FUCKING OUT!
I'm pissed off acting sad,
to make them all feel glad,
their diagnosis was right,
when really I am fooling them,
knowing it's all a load of shite,

my mind is clear,
as crystal as can be,
but only a select few see it,
and one of them is me.

Curse

Feeling depressed,
feeling so sad,
need to be brought up,
news from home'll do it,
even if it's bad,
those words aren't true,
better bad news,
than no news,
bad news is worse,
so these words are only a curse.

Curtains

Unbridled, bedazzled,
slightly half frazzled,
fuzzy brain, feels the pain,
of a night that was razzled.
Now to open the blind,
that's a curtain of a kind,
and let the world lookin in,
show me here to begin,
watchin you, watchin me,
a vague apparition that I see,
there's no solid definition,
so it joins in the melee,
for the performance to start,
the curtain is undrawn,
it's been hanging around waiting,
since the early dawn,
so don't keep them restless,
or you'll be seen as a pawn,
a sheep through your life,
with an incessant bleat,
not able to stand,
on your own two feet,
Right! You black sheep,
have you any wool?

Position's please!
Not one amongst us,
is a fool.
Open the curtains,
we'll wash them over like a wave,
then sit back, feet up,
and let the reviews rave!

Deciphered

He talked a language,
my head understood,
the stabilisation,
of my every mood,
Bipolar, Unipolar,
intermediate in between,
he covered them all,
like I've never seen.
This Doctor is sound,
why can't I have him,
or someone similar,
but defo not slim,
no harm to you doc,
but you talk a lot a cock,
with your patronizing ways,
and flickering gaze,
look me straight in the eyes,
and see the surprise,
when I'm miraculously cured,
By a shrink that's not blurred.

Depression

Are you deflated?
Down in the dumps?
Hurry up people....
Where are the pumps?
I'm sinking quite fast,
and I need some air,
Where are the people,
Who said they care?
Ah here she comes,
my lovely wife,
she'll understand me,
and give breath to my life.
Why does it always rain on me?
I'm unhappy enough,
can't you see?
But I will see clearly,
when the rain has gone,
6 years is a while,
but it's not a lifetime long.
It'll pass in a while,
chin up and be strong,

however its instigated,
look it straight in the eye,
from now and in the future,
till the day you die!

Dogs

Man's best friend,
or only for a lend,
unconditional love from below,
hail, rain, shine or snow,
Gran's companion,
or Belzebub's minion,
comfort for the night,
or a source of tremendous fright,
teeth bared when they want to,
bites worse than it bark,
loyal with every fibre of it's being,
to the smallest quark,
shapes and sizes varying,
and temperaments likewise,
howling, growling, prowling,
but see the trust that's in their eyes,
hunting, grunting, ferreting out,
smelling danger before it comes near,
hearing the signals,
that we fear to hear.

Drops

There's a house in the clearing,
dyed green with effect,
it's on the wrong cycle,
what do you expect?
Water tumbles from the roof,
of our neglected stall,
completing rotation,
that's not basic to all.
The broken fountain drinks,
from the poisoned ink well,
finalizing deals of a thirst,
that won't seem to quell.
Born not born,
not force fed life yet,
alternative thinking,
must be more than a pet.
The diet that's balancing,
chained fastly to excess,
must be given a stability,
that's comfortable with less.
We need a pyramid of thought,
that makes us equilateral,
gives us back our faith in fellow man,
enough to use each other as collateral,

an antidote so potent,
it's a permanent vaccine,
and a way of administering without dilution,
the fear of being clean.
A concentration on the circulation,
of a free windfall for expectation.
Hope has elasticity,
rubber properties that will erase the pain,
and a spring that keeps rebounding,
when you have everything to gain.

Elationships

Hi how are ye?
How's it going hi?
Pleased to meet you,
I'm doing fine,
what's your favourite colour?
Blue like the skies,
same as meself,
I've a head for heights,
but I'm partial to brown,
sort of like the earth,
very deep down,
in a way it's parallel,
yet we physically touch,
on a molecular level,
not for the impaired of vision as such meetings of minds,
of all different kinds,
we've broken them up,
is it ourselves we applaud,
but who are we,
to sit and play God?

Embalmed

They've finally arrived,
on their jet plane,
after years and years,
and again and again,
the promises cousins make,
of meeting each other,
but now they're here,
sister to sister and one another,
your looking well says the yank,
have you been embalmed?
Is the secret of life
enclosed in your hand?
Do you use the power,
to wash your body all over,
it looks timeless and ageless,
there's a sheen from your coat,
that's just like rover!

Engine ear

Would a planet made of granite,
create its own black hole?
Would the people that are living there,
have a different soul?
If they had no sky to gaze upon?
Would they let their lives just move along?
Making money day to day,
only ever stopping to pay?
No sea or tides or wind or rain,
and nothing ever to cause them pain,
With work, money and power their only vices
and nothing ever to break the ISIS,
Would they all live in complete harmony?
All thinking the same that they are all free!
Are they any different to him,
or her,
or you,
or me?
When they wonder if anyone's out there,
that is maybe just the same,
Do their eyes slip from the scoreboard,
and forget it's all a game?
Is the weight upon their shoulders,
a little more than they can stand?

And to afraid to ask for help,
they all just say they're grand.
Do their memories have an effect?
When they look forward with retrospect,
use their experience with intellect,
and share their knowledge with dialect.
So if like us,
they have the parts of the sum,
would they all realize it's a continuum.
That they each shape lives,
even with no wealth,
so why not use it for every ones health?

Epilogue

Qualified people,
to show you inside and out,
and to check out your teammates,
and see who's about,
the Durac injection,
is a yearly unravel,
for sports equipment, some coaching,
affiliation and travel,
on or off campus doesn't matter,
cause we always teach u from scratch,
just unlocking that good brain of yours,
then merely lifting the latch,
and with a face lift on Luce sports centre,
it's looking rather smart,
indoor sports,
and martial arts,
as every style in existence,
is very close to my heart,
with cardiovascular resistance,
for and against the machines,
we must learn to control them,
before they develop some jeans,
2 mile upstream,
painted better than knew,

is the ladies and men's boat club,
@ Santry avenue,
but for me, 5 mile north,
is where my hidden talent will unfurl,
the minute I see those goal posts,
and the second I touch that sacred hurl!

Eternal Itch

Itchy and scratchy,
can leave you all patchy,
the eternal itch,
from the open wound.
Swollen full of anger,
like an inflated balloon,
it's red and irritating,
will it ever fucking heal?
If they keep me locked up,
then under lock and key,
is how I'm gonna feel.
Is my nails sharp enough,
or does it need a buff,
do you think I look very tough?
On the outside I look as hard as nails or the like,
but deep on the inside,
I'm just one big sharpened spike!
So please don't anger me,
or I'll turn it into a skewer,
cos there's none more pure,
than a repentant whore.

But fuck y'all,
I'm gonna have some fun,
So I'll light my ass,
And blow y'all to Kingdom come!!!

Evolution

And so it starts,
a new beginning,
a clean sheet, fresh page,
a chance for winning,
a different song,
a brand new tune,
a future bright,
a forthcoming attraction,
in the cinemas soon,
a star of the future,
a blinding shine,
a discarder of be-grudgers,
let them whine.
A drinker of beer,
a tippler of delights,
Can you see my name?
It's up in lights,
I prefer it on the ground,
written in drunken piss,
cos i'm a down to earth guy,
you don't want to miss,
a playboy to millions,
a lover to a few,
I should only have one,

but sure what can ye do!
No money in the bank,
but piles in my arse,
I don't need the penny's,
they're just a farce.
I'll drive my ferrari,
and tell my mother not to worry!!!!

Favourite things

A favourite thing can be of many sorts,
if it's not to your liking,
well then you can abort.
If it's a song you like,
that you play over and over,
or your wee pet dog whose name is rover,
a minor pleasure in life,
not to all or everyone's liking,
but it raises a passion in you,
as in an angry Viking.
The passion and feeling,
this thing does cause,
makes you stop in your tracks,
it makes life pause.
Not just a pastime,
to while away the hours,
it could be stamp collecting,
or picking of flowers,
but it's unique to you,
and when it's unavailable,
it turns you blue,
it's a favourite thing,
or it could be plural,
like the silence of a winter's night,

somewhere rural,
it creates inner peace,
and gives you breathing space,
a break from reality,
and the whole human race!

Fianna Never Fail

All I can say,
is up Donegal!
We tried and failed,
but we did not fall,
McEniffs men,
all done us proud,
so if you're from Donegal,
stand tall and shout it loud,
our Tir Chonnaill Gladiators,
learned some rugby moves,
it didn't work this year,
but they're only finding their groves,
so watch this space,
we will rise to the top,
a skill and aggression onslaught,
that'll be impossible to stop.

Fingers

I found the solution,
but what's the problem,
the questions in the answer,
variety solves them,
now you've the information,
use it wisely,
unequivocal,
and don't be miserly,
talk till understood,
under whatever they stand,
Q and A sessions,
to beat the band,
Animalistically humble,
with a giggly growl,
laugh or maul,
on the benevolent prowl.

Fiona

I saw your thought,
I saw your mind,
Unfettered, Unfeathered,
beautiful smile.

First impressions

When you look at a face,
can you see what's inside?
The secrets beneath,
what does it hide?
Expressions of movement,
language and tone,
a flick of the eyes,
that can cut to the bone.
A smile so radiant,
it could outshine the sun,
or a cheeky little grin,
full of mischief and fun.
The windows to the soul,
are said to be the eyes,
but practice and experience,
can help them tell lies.
Actions, reactions,
rejection and attractions,
cause to concentrate,
and reasons for distractions,
say more about the soul,
than the eyes ever could,
so when you look at a face,
take in the entire attitude.

Fitness

Eat well,
drink well,
everything in moderation.
If you're not fit playing sports,
it can be a hard aul station.
Preoccupation can often be a fault,
some people lock themselves away,
as if in a vault.
You could call it determination,
but with fitness and happiness,
there's sometimes no relation,
train hard, play hard,
is the order of the day,
but don't train at all,
and you'll certainly pay,
so do a bit of both,
to promote muscle growth,
a fit body means a fit mind,
but slouch around,
and pull your wire,
you'll definitely go blind,

so get off your ass,
don't be so fucking lazy,
if you do nothing at all,
you'll go fucking crazy.

The Opportunist

Catch it when it's flying,
it's too late when it's dying,
it can be gone,
but not forgotten,
on a second chance,
there's no relying,
so when you hear the knock,
upon the door,
or it's thrown that fast,
it knocks you to the floor,
seize it, grasp it don't fumble,
and let it go,
hold it, squash it,
both hands if so needs be,
you won't regret the moment of fret,
when you open your hands and see!

Focus

Hearts and minds will meet as one,
agreeing there is more,
on it's way with morning sun,
comes the daily chore,
a grind of the mind,
the unbegrudging kind,
as we peel the orange skin rind,
to cure the bind,

And blind they are and deaf and dumb,
by accident or choice,
they lost their sense and confidence,
they failed to find their voice,
they will search and they will find,
some billion screams,
the voice of one,
throughout their dreams.
The volume of their unison,
will wake them from their slumber,
with sun on the horizon,
they'll show us their true number.

Forore

You save me from myself,
I'm in love with no-one else,
never could,
never would.

Free admission

The parking permit,
is in the post,
but I've always got some space,
and I'm a gracious host,
Phantom of the opera,
or forever a ghost,
It's now up to you,
to make the most.

For Doyler when he came to visit me.

Friends

This is all,
about life in Donegal,
Where we hate all begrudgers,
and say fuck'em all,
We live life to the fullest,
we like a life full of fun,
we work hard and play hard,
as for those who don't,
they can stick it up their bums,
Cos our motto's pretty cool,
it's all about the UMS,
there's the first one listed,
and you show it with your thumb.
We live life to the fullest,
so that's maximum,
you show the second with your index,
and take down your thumb,
this one's for empty glasses,
so it's a minimum,
and last but not least,
so bang it on your drum,
take down your index,
extend your middle finger,
and just say FUCK'UM.

Friendships

Two minds, one vision,
the peripheral watching the present,
the long and short reaching for the mission,
we're in it together,
within the titanium grip,
such a short time,
yet joined at the hip,
three legged race's are right up our street,
we'll trip everyone else,
then excel ourselves churning up the peat,
why waste oil and coal,
when there's always bi-polar,
we've more power within us than solar,
if you could bottle it up,
inside a closed cup,
you'd have more wisdom,
than in your back molar!
There's no such thing as best friends,
you have friends that are true,
that you'd lay down your life for,
and they do the same for you,
so we keep an eye on the horizon,

and one in the past,
learn from history,
and keep an open mind for the future,
and through it all - our friendship will last!!!

Fuck the models Emma

I've only just met you,
and I think you're really sound,
I love your eyes,
they're really bright and round,
I can see inside them,
a true sign of intelligence,
but this fear of being fat,
you'll have to dispense.
If you lose any more weight,
it'll destroy that lovely figure,
because contrary to woman's belief,
men prefer their ladies bigger!
What I can't figure out,
is who told you all skinny was good?
I blame the fucking supermodels,
for promoting lack of food.
All everyone needs is exercise,
because what you see and read,
is all a load of shite.
Exercise to stay in shape,
to keep you fit and keep you light,
so take care of yourself,

be nice to that body of yours,
and if people piss you off,
well fuck them,
they belong in the suirs!!

Love

Every breath I breathe,
says I love you,
you're the breathe that breaths air to my lungs,
and life to my soul.

Without you I suffocate,
and with you I float,
your love is the ocean,
on which I sail my boat.

The more I think of you,
the horizon expands,
to distant countries,
and foreign sands,
places afar,
and also at home,
for my heart is with you,
whenever I roam.

We'll sail our ship,
from shore to shore,
and we will be together,
for ever more,

our souls will find wind,
where there is none to be found,
and carry us safely along,
the most treacherous sound.

Give us a few seconds

I've something to ask ya,
have you got time Nicola,
"Just a minute,
I'll be with you in a seconda",
I know it'll be a little longer,
but the spasm won't kill ya,
they'll make you stronger,
if you're waiting for a light,
you might have to wait a few seconds,
that'll take the whole fucking night,
the phone lines are down,
depressed as can be,
a shift in power,
she wants it all you see,
I cracked the codes,
and its pissed off time for her,
so she ripped it off so quick,
it look like a blur,
but I asked her a question,
for a soothing light,
so she slowed like a sloth,
not much to my delight,
because I've no phone,
nor any fucking light!

Golf

You first strike the pose,
as everyone knows,
then check your stance,
and address the ball,
hit it with rhythm,
and watch it rise and fall,
where it lands,
depends on your direction,
and for men if it lands right,
there's a possible erection,
but woman are cooler,
because they play consistently,
without any huff,
a good shot, bad shot,
or if it lands on the rough,
they play the percentage,
not like the men,
who go for the pin,
and end up in it again.
But as the men get older,
they start loosing their balls,
and playing like woman,
makes them bang their heads of the walls!
It's a great game to play,

I love the scent of the grass,
I love playing my friends,
and kicking their ass!!
Drive for show,
and put for dough,
On the 18th,
it's the conclusive club,
a nice little gimme,
and it's into the pub.

Gone?

So is Fiona gone?
Am I like W.B Yeats?
whose Maud was Gonne?
I think gone for a while,
but not forever,
something did click,
that would take a lot to sever,
minds of a likeness,
thoughts and feelings,
that were spoken to digress,
freedom of speech,
and speak to be free,
a kindred bird without wings,
yet not into flings,
it came at a time,
which we truly needed,
and we had the feeling,
with which to feed it,
it may have been love,
for a very short time,
but she hasn't let go,
as I rightly know,
the action and not the words,
the depth in a short time,

how it all came about,
how it all occurred,
I'll move on and so will she,
we'll meet on the other side,
so as grampa said,
c'est la vie!

Happy 30th James

Death it wax beaconing my brother Môn frère
It wasn't just you I gave myself a scare
Heart was beating a million miles an hour
Height flight falling with power
I rose from reality
And the parallel verse
Its uni its bi
Who cares I'm there its terse
Happy Birthday Happy Birthday to my one and only Bru
Cheers to my sister for the cuckoo has flown its coup

Shitzo Diverse

The universe is dividing all for one dual compatibility
come out fighting your 30 now. Mc
Gregor doesn't stand a chance!

Did that tune then ultra oligarchy fulfil the plot
Its ending with love black eyes the lot
Love is strained
Love is a plot
Why so tenses
There's tae in the pot
Love in the thirties
Smells gal lour
Pig swill me hole
There's gas in the street
Where two heads meet
Ultra oligarchy I will rule it
Hands shot guided created
From unbeknownst to where
He could write from now until Christmas
You hear our thoughts
Ogden away
Door slams shut

Your Pie Hole

Pestilence bitterness of course it went in
The thoughts of being a no one
Is where to begin
Benign it's a Scara Manga
A history of violence oh no I mean aggression
Who the fuck doesn't
Welcome to the Fleadh Coel
I love the Irish
I love being me
It's the others or am I paranoid
No their afraid to be free
He faltered he's played
There loving / stealing his humour
You are on TV
Oh Wahoo wahee
Whaoooh

Her heart haith fluttered
Digging the heel
Well healed he feeled
An ode to Paddy Duffy
Your current your collected
Your lifted and laid
Is it any wonder you feel guilty your constantly splayed

Welcome to bachelorhood
Your forty years ago
The ceasefire is current
Welcome to the BBC the worlds about to blow
James Blunt surfaced again
The don't want me to have fame
Enough
Hon nuit
Moneys Money Love is life
I am a physic and I'm okay
Because I talk to boys they think I'm gay
I'm a women and that's alright He must have some money
That man wrote Flight
Young Cons the man he wrote Em&Em
Everyone's tuning in I see them connecting
Every thought and every squint
Is noted
Doted
Then torn apart
Then your brain is driving them insane

DaDa

If you believe all you hear you'll eat all you see
That's why America is so fat
Its consumer advice I am top of the tree
Inspiration detracted what's there was there before
It was burnt into me at seven whilst standing at the door
Look after the family when I'm dead and gone
Live your plan don't be a pawn
Towns cracked there going down the pan
Threatening behaviour fuck me he thran
Call me rubber duck paddling like fuck
Glengad in the heart
Charlie done a fart
Welcome to glorious a day in the sun
Oh my what a day
Croisette was fun
Tune in tune out
Love not loves now
So long the crow
Goodbye the crow
The vultures have got him
Throwing the stone to slice it in half
The greyback was lucky welcome to the gaff
Anger prevails wind in your sails
A schizoid life of course I'm afraid

Nervous gal lour
Balls no more
He's living on his own
He writtith like a black man
He write with fear
What happened to succinct
That women just dropped a tear
Welcome to the precent
Who's living my life
Welcome to Egypt
There trouble and strife
Life full of memories
Yours started in 2 11
Captains use peripheries
Young Con swings his head
No pentameter Welcome to the suck
You just got a price in your head
The whole lot can get fucked eat your meal
The sword we wield
Rice and chicken
Moving through ranks
Thanks a bunch
Back to the start
She'd have done a fart

Murder she wrote
Dads heart is in a sling
Bells 15mins early
My mama can sing

Leg Before Wicket

LGBT
LBW
Whets that you C
Fuck me in the temple
Fuck me in the street
When two Thrans meet
Writings getting bigger
Energy gone from the hand
Solely left balls in a bind
Shadow gone from the eye
Spirit from the left
Provosted on right
Finger and thumb
Press up begin
Welcome to the Oligarchs
What's there was there before
I reiterate (Its just ahh you did see it!)
I'm putting charts
Never pitt bruvers
Yap does it again
It's not his word
That's whey they refrain
They took the pride out
Because I failed not to sin

He's speaking, I put conjuring
Through the devil/Lord
Its mixed in begin
Welcome to Genius
Everyone's on the level
There's eyes fucking everywhere
Thrown in Cork
Unveiled in the street
Brides at the door come in come in
Writing everywhere
It's a catharsis of power
Frenzy of evidence
Silver screen learning
Oh know he knowth too much
Good book taken of him
Welcome to France
Where did he get the head
I would not let them in on it
Not one bloody sinner
Who'd go near that working class Heron
Learn the guitar
Bird cages ready welcome to saint martin
He threatened my son no you treat him well

You keep on writing the giants of fell
Fall upon my shoulder Fall upon my Knife
Ni neirt go cur le cheile
Piss taking we will see

Out to Annoy

Out to annoy
Out to rule
Resilience prevails
Who looks the fool?
Right foot feels the soul
Tip toeing in reverse
Everything they are doing
Is fucking perverse
Sadness prevails
When I think of the past
Gun to the head
Give it a blast
Kurt Cobain I feel your pain
Ronny Drew I feel the strain
Guinness for breakfast
Buck fast for lunch
Letterkenny General thanks a bunch!

Fucked up fubared beyond control
Resilience is paramount
This towns in a hole
Party animal central
The naughtiest are gone
We are in our teens

People moving away they are busting there spleens
We are the God damn Spartans
I trained in Sparta
What's the matta?
Your on the mat
Kate Lafferty took my Dad away

Oligarchy

The mood changes with sound I just felt the knife
Wing taken from my back
Arterial connected in disconnects from my right side
The neck he's in swinging a beautiful
Swimmingly great
That girls got red hair
(God damn it)
Seen in the air
Writing on the wall ah hair
I care (u)
Obviously needs it
Viagra jokes his
Subliminally blind
That's why he fizz

Irma

To Richard Branson
The whole point is to hear it
Words fly of the page
That was bugs welcome to the spark
That's mammy outside
Oh wait it's not
Dark and dusky morning on a plane bound for nowhere
Cross hair
I am down with
Your ready
Take the fucking
Reep what you sow
In an ellocuint fashion
A sword a nife
Who needs the Kay"
Weetabix is tasty
Words are at play
The poet named Wordworth

Alota money

Lears
Fucking clueless
Bound tight lyin in the dirt
Gets up and starts walking has he no memory of the plot
Well yes he does
Welcome to memorandum

Tumour (easter) this fucker is loaded
slow down your going to fast
Has he got a women?
Benign belay be writing what we day
Interrupt flow freely no commas or stops
It has an effect have they lost the plot
This shit is genius its exactly what they done
All involved dont want to hear
Its all pure lunacy
Whos the fucking man
Is he to get mercy?
A beat you to the punch
haha nah nah
He hears he feels
uniform is needed
GAA lower
Foclair Humpty Dumpty

Well he has put himself back together
Heirplay
Fucked up fubared beyond recogniation
Lift him commas are coming
Love lift fear behoven
Feared unbehoven
Internet in the brain
You just got your knee back
Burned in feel the heat
Cross to bear
Weird at black cross in the air
If this is scitzo?
Then Im all for it
Nambi pambi
smoke in the air
The writing is senseiful
Booze hounds will get it
Piece in the membrane
Welcome to genetitist
This is crappola
Whos the judge
Welcome to Niall
To old for styling
Welcome to Joanna

Ya good thing ya
Out and about having fun
Tinkers in town
There already here

I'm a poet yeah why you?
Got a problem with that?
Jesus wept!
Love in a puddle,
total avoidance,
they all can scram,
the love in a bucket,
welcome to Nantucket,
whale blubber my hole,
that fucker is heavyweight,
me balls he opinions galore,
that guy fucked you,
he's her fucked senseless,
Shoa moan mutha fucka

173

Keep on writing welcome to
DeWett,

that's from Dan,
take him for a beer,
that kid needs a break,
yeah you,
I can see it in his eyes,
deathly silent rigormortis,
rigid solid
No rest for the wicked,
paper is scare..sce

Joyce country, gay in a band
You'll get no peace and that's
(eyes directed towards the cup(lyons tea)) from
a lion. Why what he stills
hold grudges
meet & fear,
Nat one welcome to the fingers,
clasp I love you,
you put fear in con,
love life and fruit of the loom whom,
hierarchy, just love life.

Start it with moet

A sparkle to the day,
drunk or not,
the mamosa was gorgeous
have you lost the plot?
you see it both sides,
you're mentally aware,
ah hair ah care,
subjew down trodden,
mentally off track,
and he's back,
it's galloping in,
Con's giving it power.
you are in fucking grey skill,
Upper L.a
East side west side,
They all tuning,
he's getting his nutts
squeezed,
Ephemeral thought,
Dust in the wind,
that's what they had planned,
the whole lots in the bin

They're watching they love you,
Smoke veils and threats,
tr,
testing testing one
two,
Wan two,
Con can sing YOUR HEARTS
OUT TO THE GLORY OF THE
MAN RABBIE WILLIAMS,
ya man of course ye can
Orlath I love you,
Dan anthracite,
Dust mortimer don't fart.

Hear & Now

Where am I?
Am I here?
I know I am,
but others fear,
but don't worry ma,
because I do listen to you,
don't think I ignore,
because I do what I do,
I'll take it handy,
keep the head,
but people piss me off,
and I see the mist of red,
this does not mean,
that I am still high,
but the apron strings need cut,
I need to fly,
so I ask you please,
it's hard enough,
let me go,
and find my way outta the rough.

Hick!!!

What do you believe?
The questions asked,
is the answer received?
Do I know?
Or don't I care?
All those questions,
with no answer,
has the drink got a grip,
or can I rip,
free from the noose,
that it holds me in?
Am I ashamed?
Is it a sin?
Of course I am,
but is it the time,
we're living in?
So many around me,
drink the same,
how can you judge,
with them in the same vain?
My mind is strong,

but will it remain?
Only I know it will,
because I'm so thick,
possibly because I'm a straight country hick!!!

Homeless

Lying in the street with nothing to eat,
My eyes pouring over the rain,
locked up in a shed without any bed,
tripping on acid,
outta my head,
at first I faultered,
then I squared,
but the sound that I saw was something I heard.
Eyes playing tricks,
rats in the mix,
fear and loathing and lots of foreboding,
awake in the morning,
a pain in the heart,
10 quick press-ups,
good for a start,
push the embellizm out if that how it works,
no-one to help,
we all have our quirks.
Now for day and somewhere to reside,
I'm not going home because a mental home I can't abide...

Humility

It's everyone's,
it's mine and yours,
it's in a gift,
and in small gestures,
it's bowing down,
in grateful praise,
or gracious acceptance,
or simply to raise
the lowly, the needy,
those of no belief,
it's in the eyes,
of the petty thief.
It's underestimated,
so appreciate it.

Con

All in a lifetime as Daddy does say,
do I go with the flow,
and in God we pray?
Or grab the bull by the horns,
and decide my own fate!
The first one sounds easy,
the last one sounds real,
stand up and be counted,
show them your steel!
It's an individualistic attitude,
to set you apart,
to find your own path and make your mark,
self-fulfillment through selfless acts,
to be held in the same light,
and respected as he,
too much to ask for?
I have to wait and see,
misguided opinions on other peoples thoughts,
how others see you as you see yourself,
what I've craved for as boy,
and now as man,

is the respect from others,
that I think I've earned,
but not as a madman or wildcard in the pack,
but as a serious contender who's on the right track!

I don't love Lucky

Fuck him left and fuck him right,
fuck him sideways,
the fucking bender,
he won't be so smart,
when I put him in a blender.
I thought to be a shrink,
you had to be bright,
but from what I can see,
he needs two arseholes,
to get rid of all his shite.
He'll rue the day,
he ever lied to me,
I'll fuck him up good,
just watch and see.
Spoke to like a child,
enjoys the patronize,
well just watch him tremble,
when I cut him down to size.
I know farmers at home,
who'd keep him for his shite,
he speaks from both ends,
day and night,
he should start a workshop,
teaching the art of manure,

189

it's a viral condition,
and therefore no cure.
No eye to eye contact,
therefore shifty and sly,
well fuck you Lucky,
here's your job,
kiss it goodbye!

If dreams could come true

If dreams could come true,
what would we do?
Would mine affect yours?
Then we'd all be in the suirs,
forget all that shit,
we can dream it'll never happen,
non-conflicting dreams,
that'll leave God flapping!!
The devil will dance,
in the heart of the earth,
he'll throw his fork over his shoulder,
and off he'll prance,
more fuel for the fire,
like a burning black tyre,
but it's not for dreamers,
as you might suspect,
it's for the shrimp on the barbie,
and the devils sweet dialect,
Oh what a party,
we're going to have,
for the beer competitions,
we'll split the teams in half!!
My God! Said a man,
"if anyone can, lucifer,

you certainly can",
Gods here too?
What do you mean?
This is blasphemous,
it's downright obscene,
you're in on this together,
said the nosey old guy,
fuck off said God,
while I finish my rye!
With a slurp and a sup,
and with one swift hand,
he crushed the cup!
He turned to the guy,
and said to him,
"It's all a game,
don't you see?"
Just keep your eye on the scoreboard,
Or you'll be closer to me!

I'm.....

I'm a wanderer,
I'm a ponderer,
I'm a loner,
I'm a moaner,
I'm a suggestor,
I'm a molester,
I'm a joker,
I'm a stoker,
I'm a broker,
I'm a choker,
I'm a mooner,
I'm a crooner,
I'm a fighter,
I'm a writer,
I'm a lover,
I'm a cover,
I'm a shielder,
I'm a yielder,
I'm a counter,
I'm a mounter,
I'm a canter,
I'm a ranter,
I'm a raver,
I'm a paver.

Imprisonment

Every minute is like an eternity,
have you ever been locked up?
It can be quite scary!
Freedom is the one of many things I hold dear,
although normally joking...
about this I'm quite sincere,
if you don't have your freedom,
what have you got?
A city full of cars,
but an empty parking lot!
They can get in,
but we can't get out,
you can walk to the gate,
but then right turn about!
Back in your box,
jack the lad,
I don't care if you're just happy,
this'll make you sad!
Well you know what?
No matter how they try,
You won't change me,
I don't care how you swot,
pearls of wisdom,
rolling down your face,

I don't care if we've only met,
up where I come from,
we call it sweat,
so sweat all you want,
gimme those pills,
I'll sit and I'll smile,
at the world sitting on the window sills,
it's not them I'm after,
it's just life's thrills!!!

In the army now!

You going to the army,
are you fucking barmy?
Do you need to do tests?
Nah ya fool! Just turn up with all vests,
whats that you say?
it's not like the FCA,
we've to bring our own!
What about the grass?
When we're goin mown,
I prefer fools carrying arms,
Is that what we stand for?
Well if that's what you say,
then that's what you do!
But your ass is that wide,
the chair will come too,
so shut your fat mouth,
or ya gonna feel pain,
drop and give me twenty,
then do it again,
go grab your gun,
and not the one between your legs,
assume the position and hit them pegs,

think of them as brits and bite their tits,
we're preparing for war and it'll be far from civil,
we'll kick their fucking asses,
and let them drown in the drivel.

Inbetween Dreams

There's too much time,
spent between dreams,
even if they come true,
time spent planning,
anticipating,
time spent on a fair few,
and sometimes time,
between dreams,
lasts longer than they last themselves,
and it extends,
to such extent,
that
there are dreams no longer,
without any themes,
that make ya stronger,
strength of mind,
and courage of conviction,
dreams that'll last,
from the obscurest prediction.

It is as it is

The red hand of Ulster says No!
But the green hand of Ireland says yes,
but before we argue,
let us digress,
it was ours before,
and it still is ours now,
so when you think about it,
why the big row?
you stole it from us,
under a false pretence,
we had depression from oppression,
and limited defence,
it's a different story now,
from those by-gone days,
we're all shining bright,
just look @ our rays,
every corner of the earth,
has a little Irish in them,
your empire is no more,
there's very few left for you to condemn,
our point is made,
so give us it back,
if not my vengeance,
you will exact,

there's many more like me,
who'll support the 6 counties expense,
I hope it doesn't go too far,
but attack is the best form of defence.

Joe!

So joe!
Say it ain't so,
fuck it man,
it'll soon be over,
so just let it blow,
over your head,
gone with the wind,
if I act normal is that a sin?
Well if it is,
you gotta ask me,
do I care?
Cos I know when I'm angry,
I really scare,
get back in your cell til I lock you up,
you tell'um joe,
the cheeky pup,
tell him to shift his ass,
or you'll fuck him up,
so take it easy and if you get it nice,
then do a good job,
and fuck him twice!!
So hometime now,
piece of pie,
like sugar and spice!!

Just one minute

I hear a voice in the morning,
and the evening,
the radio and the CD's make me feel sane again.
But if I tell the doctors and the nurses,
they'll drug me up for absurdity,
so I should have been home,
yesterday, yesterday,
Irish homes,
take me home,
to the place where I BELONG,
East Donegal, mountain mama,
Irish roads, take me home.
The majority of them are nice,
but as the saying goes,
it only takes one bad apple to spoil
what once was delicious slice.
But don't be impatient,
in fact I know I am,
but they're so fucking slow,
cos if they were in the race,
with the turtle and the hair,
they'd never win it,
cos every thing you ask for,
is in a minute.

God forbid they say 5,
cos then you're truly fucked,
one takes an hour,
so 5 will be next week,
and probably by then,
you'll be dead or very week!

Just the one

The clouds were spilling rain,
I'd gone for a pint,
and had 10 again,
when I had the first one,
it started to fizzle,
sure I thought to myself,
I'll wait till it stops,
fire us up another one there,
I can smell those hops,
4,5 and 6,
it was raining bricks,
I said to the barman,
that looks heavy,
I'm not going out in that,
this'll be my lucky 7th bevvy,
I drank number 8,
as quick as I could,
cos I could see it in the barman,
he was in the closing mood,
so 9 and 10,
I ordered together,
I'll drink them and be happy,
whatever the weather.

King prawns

Don't blame it on me,
don't blame it on the moonlight,
don't blame it on the good times,
blame it on the loony,
big wheels keep on turning,
does your conscience bother you?
Clear you mind,
absolve your sins,
step aside,
we're coming through,
you're either for us,
or against,
you decide,
Cause we're about to conquer,
then divide,
by peaceful means,
and forceful ways,
so tomorrow can be every bodys todays.

KowL Oon Krazy

Lets meet @ high noon,
any earlier is to soon,
and when we kick your ass,
you can pick up those jaws of glass,
well fuck you,
I'll just do,
that sliver really brings out your eyes,
fooled you all along,
I was Bruce lee in disguise,
right here in St. Pats,
hiding under the mats,
bequeathing your suicide prize!

Leaving

I caught it,
I got it,
it was the last one I looked at,
I should've looked there first,
I've made it now in seconds flat,
leaving the craic behind,
but it's only the start of what's to come,
it's the top rung of one ladder,
and the bottom of another one,
these are ladders without snakes,
to bring you undone,
they cleanse with each step,
a filtration system that's second to none,
so we are never leaving,
just enjoy life's journey of fun!

Life

I am the greatest,
I am the best,
back me into a corner,
and I'll end your quest.
With every inch of my body,
and every thought in my mind,
I'll fight tooth and nail,
until I'm deaf dumb and blind,
If it's a test of strength,
and you want a real fight,
try stopping the sunshine turning into night,
if it's a jealous attack that's to try and whittle down,
then you'll always wear the head,
that's too big for the crown.
A reactive response,
to the threat that you perceive,
will leave you entangled,
in the web that you weave.
When you look to yourself,
at the threat that's within,
basic instincts of survival,
is where to begin.
Resentment of control,
and fear of its loss,

is meal you feel made tastier,
by an adequate bitter sauce.
Indigestion,
then congestion,
followed when not chewed,
so when offered a slice,
of friendly advice,
think from where it's viewed.

Little Hitleress

What's the fucking story?
What is it with you today?
Did I do something wrong?
And I'm being punished in this way?
If I did it wasn't intentional,
but where the Jesus are we?
A facility for correctional?!

Lives

When watching your face,
I have to stifle my roar,
I can feel it coming,
the blood rush in our veins,
the head on collision,
of two speeding trains,
I squeeze you tight,
you bite my chin,
nothing else in the world matters,
but our feelings within,
the trains collide,
we both explode,
we're floating in space,
with no fixed abode,
the sky is happy,
it screams out Amen,
we're the moon and the sun,
together again,
for eternity.

Eternal Itch

Itchy and scratchy,
can leave you all patchy,
the eternal itch,
from the open wound,
swollen full of anger,

Love

What is love?
Is it sent from the heaven?
Or dormant in the heart?
Awaiting activation,
amalgamation with your other part.
When this is done,
it's then it does start,
every second of every minute,
the whole day through.
It gets harder all the time,
without seeing you,
yet when we're together,
it's eternal bliss,
our love and senses soar exponentially,
the independent body might abscond,
but the heart follows mentally,
the trees and the grass,
and the lovely flowers,
are part and parcel,
of Gods powers,
this gives me love,
whether it's hail rain or shine,
like drilling a hole,
in Ethiopa to get water from the mine,

I truly believe,
it turns the world in a spin,
but you must work in harmony,
and give love a chance to win!

Ma petite cherie

I feel it lifting but I'm taking it slow,
no more leaping before I know,
I have the laughter of a grafter,
but my banter's at a canter,
I'm reading the rhyming dictionary,
and playing mental pictionary,
my scribbles at a dribble,
but I want to hear it roar,
I want to be happy,
I want to be me,
I want to feel companionship,
that'll set me free,
less than half my life,
without a wife,
but who is this girl?
My fantasy....
Without a boast, there is many that care,
but that which attracted was non-conformity,
it gave them hope,
some dispelled the rope.
I changed their outlook on reality,
But I am lost and feel I can't be found,
I'm trying to find my centre and touch the ground,
I touch the earth, but can't feel the taste,

surely all I've done is not a waste,
I've lived a movie in my own minds eye,
I'm on the brink of a crossroads,
and I don't know why?
I'm on a trampoline with mile long springs,
waiting to rise and test my kevlar wings,
I don't want to miss it,
what a terrible fear,
is my life on hold?
what am I waiting to clear?
the smoke I've created,
is blinding my eyes,
my heart wants to move on but maintain the ties,
Love is a bastard,
I love it to death,
I try not to think of her with every breath,
this isn't her fault and neither is it mine,
but in the truth,
there is wine.
It's all my will trying not to spill this all out into a glass,
it would be nice with a few cubes of ice,
but it was her that capped the gas.
My spirit was escaping with no anticipating,
wandering it blew into a paranoid wind,

as long as the juice was there I did not care,
I could squeeze from any excuse,
all rhyme no reason whatever the season,
I was just brimming to let all hell break loose,
so I calm the edge with an eternal pledge,
and I use her as my muse,
but I didn't mask,
did she want the task,
is that why I fumble and stumble and confuse?
Am I writing history in a man-made mystery,
to which the answer eludes?
and every time it hurts, in fits and spurts,
I can't blame the frustration that intrudes,
She's stated her case, face to face,
but why do I see eyes that are hidden?
for if the truth that I feel is actually real,
then God please let them do their bidding,
or is it all fake?
And I just keep stepping on that rake,
oblivious to reputation and pride,
but I wish it so,
that we'll stand toe to toe,
and eye to eye as husband and bride.

Maybe?

Thinking of feelings,
do they happen through time?
Or flash in an instant?
And start crowding your mind?
Never wanted someone so badly,
that I can taste and touch and smell,
when I close my eyes and think,
and for a while I feel so happy,
but when I open I'm in hell,
I want you here right by my side,
and snuggling in my ear,
to feel safe and know that'll I protect,
and that you need never have a fear.
I know it's hard right at this time,
for me to be away,
but the only consolation is,
that you and I are here to stay!

Mind

Another day close to you,
Is how I feel with everything I do,
If it passes the time,
and occupies my mind,
then I'll do it,
just to ease the longing for you.

Monica

Hey Monica,
you're like a harmonica,
you bring music to my ears.
The only problem is it makes them bleed,
I didn't expect you to look at my poem,
cos you probably can't even read.
I'd say you're lucky,
I'm not a fighter,
It doesn't surprise me,
you don't carry a lighter.
But if you continue as you are,
your life will rise in flames,
but fuck you,
what odds is it to me,
It's all the same,
as they say at home,
you won't see it from my house,
but there's no need to look,
or talk down to people,
like they're a louse,
It's easier to be nice,
than it is to be not,
I believe you treat everyone with respect,

I don't expect a lot.
But it's your life so fuck you,
And if you stay on that path,
It'll turn into POO!!!

The Moon

Through misty glass,
staring at the moon,
listening to the soft beat,
of my favourite tune,
thinking of you,
as the clouds drift past,
knowing the darkness,
will not last,

through time and persistance,
the light will shine through,
just like our love,
and my longing for you,
in the shadow again,
as I continue to gaze,
once again it shines strong,
to dazzle and amaze,
those who were in doubt if it would,
are proven wrong,

for in the shadows life may cast,
our love will last,
as long as the moon shines on,
the silvery path to eternity,

is where our love never ends,
we will grow old together,
and take what life sends,
To young? To old?
To soon? Too late?

There's no set time,
or given date,
two souls combined,
can never be parted,
by distance or time,
or waters uncharted,
the join is seamless,
it cannot be found,
like the start of a wave,
or the end of a sound,
from two souls to one,
the journey's begun,
I feel the tingling,
that says you're the one,
I'm the happiest and securist,
that I've ever been,
and when we make love,
you take me to places,

that I've never seen,
I let myself go,
like never before,
and each time we come there,
I want to see more,
the sensation is the most beautiful,
that I've ever felt,
and when I look in your eyes,
I feel my heart melt,
it brings a lump to my throat,
and a tear to my eye,
and all my will not to cry,
tears of joy,
for thoughts untold,
but through action and time,
they begin to unfold,
our love will shine,
in all its glory,
through the test of time,
as a never ending story!

Much ado about a nothing

If you weren't mad,
before you came in,
it'll slowly ambush you,
the longer you stay,
the price is freedom,
and boredom and you'll certainly pay!
No stimulus only the nurses,
there's nothing to do,
and eventually they just say fuck you,
I see they get pissed off as well,
but they can go home,
we're left irritated and frustrated as hell,
with all the cameras,
and the constant eyes and ears,
the constant attention is to allay their fears.
It's like big brother,
without the votes and money and the end,
but it's their reputation,
they have to defend.
What drugs are you on?
Oh that's a colourful blend!
Has it made a difference?
Well neither to me!

It feels like jail,
where one and all are guilty free!
So we'll go with the program,
and suck it and see!

Nail on the head

The do's and don'ts of life's wills and won'ts,
Will they?
Won't they?
Don't they know hey?
It's their hay day,
do it now,
before it's too late,
don't look to other people,
2 judge your mental state,
be yourself,
off the shelf,
and sometimes off the wall,
stand tall and be proud,
because you are answering your call.

Ni neart go cur le cheile

The Spartans fell like leaves from the sky,
so defiant in death,
they did not die,
their remains sowed the seeds,
for generations to come,
to unite as a Nation,
and Stand alone as One.
Basically unique,
their system was designed,
to use fear of the unknown,
as a communal bind,
excellence was encouraged,
men knew their place in a marriage,
and wise words from a woman,
they would never disparage.
They fought for preservation,
and taught common sense,
and when they had a common goal,
they didn't sit on the fence.
They had pride with temperance,
all information was pooled,
and as a nation they were destined,
to be wisely ruled.

Their kings were the bravest,
and compassionate among all,
who fought form the front,
with the ANCESTRAL call.

Niamh

Life and strife,
trouble in a bubble,
but it's your little sphere,
and for most,
it's something they hold dear.
It's fragile and valuable,
and quite easy to bust,
so if you feel its over,
can't take anymore,
well out with the rope,
and then you must!
Personally I feel,
it's the cowardly option,
think of your parents,
of your brother and sister,
and dead in heaven,
and how much you missed her,
if not for yourself,
why put them through it?
It's the ultimate in selfishness,
when you DIY or BBQ it,
because the aspect of things,
that are most important to us,
are often clouded and shrouded,

in a veil of dust.
Ashes to ashes,
or jumping off bridges,
intentional car crashes,
chicken shit fuckers,
get over your strife,
just find your positon,
in this wonderful life!

No Name

Can you see what I see?
Feel what I feel?
The perception is different,
from one to the next,
it's all in the delivery,
composition of the text,
accent, affliction, affectation,
from the belly past the teeth,
is there any such thing,
as a decorative wreath?
People are dead,
but not forgotten,
is my true belief,
so I can sit back and relax,
in the quiet satisfaction of my relief.

O'Donnell

Motto: Under this sign you shall conquer.
The O'Donnells are one of the most eminent families
whose forefather was Niall of the Nine Hostages.
Tirconnell, meaning "Connell's territory" (now
Donegal) was their base, and from Domhnaill (world
mighty) they took their name. Their Chieftains were
inaugurated on the Rock of Doon near Letterkenny.
Theirs is a history of battle. They built strongholds
around Donegal and defended themselves
first from their neighbours, the O'Neills, and
then, in a losing battle, from the Tudors.
As a youth the O'Donnells heir, the great Red Hugh,
was abducted and imprisoned in Dublin castle. His
escape through the snow-covered Wicklow mountains
is one of the great sagas. He was the leader in the
Triumphant battle of the Yellow Ford, but died
in Spain following the exodus after Kinsale.
The O'Donnells established an Austrian line with a
Major General Henry Count O'Donnell. Count Joseph,
his son, was finance minister following Napoleon's
depridations. Another O'Donnell account was aide-de
camp to the Emperor Franz Josef. Their kinsman reached
the highest rank in Spain - Prime Minister in 1858.

Many O'Donnells have been illustrious churchmen, including the "Apostle of Newfoundland" and Cardinal Peter O'Donnell in Ireland. Their present chieftain is a Franciscan missionary whose heir will come from the duke of Tetuan's family in Spain.

And I am Con O'Donnell the poet without a mental illness determined to take down Bipolar and expose the big pharma for what they really are....a money making racket!

Old and why's?

If youth is wasted on the young,
then surely air is wasted on the lung,
from the old and wise,
the young and the why's?
Cloak and dagger,
fear of knowledge to impart,
because if you tell me too much,
I might know more than you,
you old fart,
knowledge is the fodder,
that makes kids minds broader,
it's the name of the game,
to teach what we learn,
for some kids it's a chore,
for other's they yearn,
so they tell what they know,
because there's no better feeling,
than watching their young mind hit the ceiling,
and watching them grow.

Paperback

Within these paper walls,
I learned not to trip,
on the pride that falls,
it has my ego contained,
my elation restrained,
and all of my faculties,
healthfully sustained.

Paperwork

Within these paper walls,
I learned not to trip,
on the pride that falls,
it has my ego contained,
my elation restrained,
and all of my faculties,
healthfully sustained.

Group therapy - one line each

Party hats

Another year gone,
we stick them on our heads,
always so small and cute,
sometimes as night caps in our beds,
let's all sing a happy party song,
No-one knows the words,
before we know they'll all be gone,
what will the year bring?
Buddha bangs his gong.
With the partiers in their throng,
some of them stripey,
in a mood where nothing seems wrong,
they don't stop to question why?
As in ecstasy they fly,
higher than their minds can ever perceive,
Are you Niamh?
Open your minds and hands to receive,
open your hearts and you'll never grieve,
pretell why fret,
surrounded by beauty how can we forget,
it's not a big stone where everything is set,
it's more of a river to which eternity flows,
it's got its own trade winds that perpetually blows.
16th day of August 2003

Picture perfect

Can something really be picture perfect?
Because every time you look at it,
it invokes a different effect,
so maybe it's not the picture,
it's more about the mood,
the angle and perspective,
of each and every time you stood,
the landscapes of the mountains,
two men on the move standing still,
they're stopped mid-stride,
are they dragging their turf or making a still?
Well we are all in lovely Ireland,
so let's stack all the bloody turf,
then go and drink our fill.

Player/Manager

They say fame and fortune,
is all about timing,
and poems and songs,
are all about rhyming,
what if all this thinking,
was turned on its head,
would you be up for a revolution,
if I told you a secret that some might dread,
it's not a bad thing,
it's really pretty good,
now I'm not kissing your ass,
from the off that must be understood,
I see these young girl/boy bands,
singing about shit they know nothing about,
and it's not their fault,
it's just whoever has the clout,
so I decided to myself,
unbeknownst to anyone,
that I'd hide myself till thirty,
then I'd knock on the door and in I'd come,
as you know yourself,
the reason you left the band,
it was becoming less inspiring,
going through the motions,

and kind of somewhat bland,
so I gave myself to thirty,
to make history of my own,
and a lifetime of material,
that would surely keep me going,
but now I'm 26 and I feel I've reached that place,
to write, sing songs and dance,
with my audience of the human race,
I'm sure you're wondering by now,
why the hell I'm writing to you?
the reasons pretty simple,
it's because you're starting a new,
you'll be open to new ideas,
not just that,
but you'll teach me some,
unlike some in your business,
inflicted with verbal diarrhoea,
full of shit up to their armpit,
that's not what I want,
I'll keep my feet on the ground,
which I believe you and your good wife have done,
so if I do my stuff,
will you make me No. 1???

Pole

If you say Uni,
doesn't that mean everyone?
I forget who I told,
somebody said somebody,
anyone, someone,
so why when about the polar,
3 halves it's shared as one?
You've up polar,
down polar,
Bipolar being 2,
and,
Unipolar being one,
so how can Uni be everyone?
anyone, who one, do one,
Then just jump right back,
saying fuck this!
It's not what I wanted,
only as one when we were one,
the last time it happened,
was it flaunted?
We conquered the pole,
so to Columbus and to backpackers,

we're now all a united whole!
Pole united could be our Gaelic team,
on my journey here,
I thought of Tom creen.

Pourqoui pas

They must be mad,
they know no reason why,
everyone here is not all bad,
although the doc's all say we're mad,
we may @ times be quiet sad,
then @ other times fly that makes us glad,
when all the cards are down,
and the money's in,
frantically swinging from high to low,
I'm taking to song. So?
Hurry up we've not got all night Eamonn,
Life is not so shite,
GOODNITE!

Radiation

When you look in the mirror,
what do you see,
is it a true reflection,
that's felt within thee?
All these problems and issues,
bottled up inside,
bursting at the seams,
yet trying to hide,
so here's a thought,
why not do what the mirror just did,
slide your baggage along the reflection,
to where the emanations are hid,
cleanse your body,
free your mind and soul,
get closure on that bad boy,
put him back in his box,
and nail the lid.

Reason?

What's it all about?
This life of ours?
It twists in turns,
and sometimes sours,
sometimes slow,
then the speed of light,
no matter your problem,
no matter your plight,

takes the feet from under you,
then gives you the wings to fly,
moves you to tears,
then laugh till you cry,

So what's it all about?
The answer's there is none,
to make you scream and shout,
But surely there's a reason,
for what's done and intended?
Continue you plans,
until they're up-ended?
Or don't plan at all,
and come what may,

ignore all advice and direction,
no matter what they say?

That would not do,
cause then you'd drift,
and in no time at all,
you'd be on the heavenly lift,

so give yourself your own reason,
for this life you lead,
and if you get good advice,
then surely take heed,

But if you still seek the reason,
a simple one will suffice,
don't worry it's just fate,
and not the role of the dice.
3 x haloperidol 10mg
3 x Serenace 10mg
Lithium 20mg(400ml)

Relax

Relax and feel good,
take your drugs,
it'll lighten your mood,
Oops a daisy,
we gave you the wrong ones,
golly gosh,
it made you crazy,
sorry about that,
my mistake,
it's funny how it made your body,
rattle like a snake,
brain is spinning,
it won't stay still,
it's okay though,
we have for you a downer pill,
we'll strike a balance,
through trial and error,
again don't worry,
but you won't know your own reflection,
in the bathroom or mirror,
but it's good for you,
cos we know best ;),
you might not know it,
but we are in the business of reading minds,

and we don't like your happiness,
you're to full of zest,
well I say fuck you,
fuck them,
and burn the Rest!

Revelation

Footprints glowing,
as my mind keeps growing,
the path ever changing,
the distance ever ranging,
360's the direction,
no need for election,
outsides the insides reflection,
and it remains the same on closer inspection,
A heartfelt search,
idiosyncratic research,
absolved of my sins,
regaining my wings and my fins,
for the journey that lies before me,
through land and sea,
sounds and snow follow me,
I'm starting to see,
the woods and the tree,
the one hand clapping,
without flapping or slapping,
it fell without noise,
it fell without noise,
and thankfully missed me.
Therapy!

Room with a view

I see an elephant through it,
I'd like to find if this was true,
skip me come back to me when it's easier,
what amazes me,
the elephant had escaped from the zoo,
he was a curious creature,
looking for something to do,
turns out not to be true,
but I argue that it is true,
but what do I know?
I live in a shoe,
they've confiscated the laces,
but it don't matter,
there ain't no traces,
this evening I'm not at the races,
but I put a few down,
just for the places,
and I couldn't help looking at all the unfamiliar faces,
for deep down I felt like I had all the
ACES.

Safety in numbers

My safe, your safe,
we're all safe together,
how safe is safe safe?
Your safe or my safe?
Lucky safe stroked,
that bit of white heather,
life can be funny,
and that blood can be runny,
thought I as he ate,
the feet of the bunny,
the luckier I practice,
the luckier I get!
You'll never meet one luckier than me,
I am the one,
you'll never forget!

SandyAndy

Like a fox,
she walks,
without a care,
stops for nothing,
a shout of "who goes there?!"
She's SandyAndy,
with the lustrous coloured hair,
a sheen and shine,
and a smile that would win,
an attractive face,
with the fluff on her chin,
from a shaky start,
with the pound as a home,
to a dwelling place,
she can call her own,
lady of the manor,
her slender long legs stride,
with a tail like a gown,
that shows assurance,
not pride,
she's an equal in the famly,
so don't forget,
she's one of you,
not just a pet.

Scratch

The taxi awaits,
@ the Golden gates,
inviting, enticing,
weaving and splicing,
thoughts in my mind,
of the escape kind,
but I know there's no point,
because when you're eventually caught,
you're back in the joint,
the decks are cleared,
and you start from scratch,
it's all a game,
it's just a match,
keep your head down,
and an eye on the scoreboard,
you've plenty of time to recover,
that you can afford.

Seacape

Early morning rise,
the sun in my eyes,
the brightness in the light,
sets the clouds on fire,
and lays a golden path,
on a sea that's swelling higher,
no matter if you stand or sit,
your perspective or your view,
the mood for the day is always set,
just like the morning tune!!

Sexually frustrated

Not even a fondle,
a feel in the dark,
the tiniest of touches,
as small as a quark?
Pourquoi pas?
Oh la la!

Should....

Should I rest?
Should I try my best?
Should I shine?
Should I have some wine?
Should I read?
Should I speak out loud?
Should I come down?
Should I descend from the cloud?
Should I float?
Should I stand?
Should I take a boat?
Should I land?
Should I walk?
Should I run?
Should I spread the word?
Should I smoke the gun?
Should I test?
Should I jest?
Should I just wait,
Till the time has come

*Friendship
Loyalty
Predictability
Trippin
Six*

Lying in the sand as far as the eye can see,
hot to touch, the waters far to reach,
I'll run with light feet,
on this crowded BEACH,
when I threw the party,
I thought I'd get a few,
I never could have imagined with a whip,
I'd have so people,
to honour me with their FRIENDSHIP,
They're here for a good time not a long time,
embarrassed as I am,
they treat me like royalty,
pledge their support,
and give me their LOYALTY,
People are cool and all like variety,
a certain askewness and respectability,
that' a mile from the norm,
and only when needed then PREDICTABILITY,

the fires lit,
and the bar-b's on,
those slices of new life,
we'll soon be flippin,
and a perspective that's new is needed,
cause reality is TRIPPIN!

Snakes & Dragons

To come here in the first place was a beautiful mistake,
for the first time in my life I've let
the Dragon eat the Snake,
It squirmed it wormed,
it tried to wriggle it's way free,
but the Dragon had a grip on it,
better than me,
so tight it'll hold,
never to unfold,
till the day I die,
or at least till I'm old,
Unforeseen friendships forged for the future fate,
late night discussions where we all debate,
It's a big discussion so call it a mass debate,
where we all come together,
and demonstrate,
our cunning linguistics are plain to see,
the sides to the argument are always three,
triangulation has so many uses,
from navigation to fire,
combine them all together for navigation with fire higher,
Higher than life is not a possible state,
neither is perfection,
but I'm coming close at this rate,

I've met so many people now true friends of mine,
whom I'd sit in any company with non-alcoholic wine,
They're smart,
they're funny,
and so god damned good looking,
they all just ooze charisma,
that would have jealous people puking,
But I'm one of them,
so it's not us that has the problem,
it's you with your glue,
trying to stick labels on us like them.

Snatchet

Bereft of personality,
when personality is key,
subtract the drugs,
and you'll still find me.
You've gotta make an allowance,
for my happy go lucky ambience,
but I won't put up with this shit forever,
so someone will soon shout for an ambulance.
I'll say one thing for free...Fuck you!!
It won't be for me,
so show me you've studied,
how to avoid your nose being bloodied,
Or are you a sheep or robot?
Put together with a socket and ratchet,
Cos if you don't show me soon,
I'll dismantle you and your dreams,
with a big fucking hatchet!!
So fuck you motherfuckers,
When I see my chance for freedom,
I'm gonna snatchet!!!

Sown

I'm a schitzophrenic,
me too!
Now where both stuck in here,
what do we do?
What the movies portray,
is totally wrong,
if it was entered in the oscars,
they'd receive a gong.
It's hard to explain,
but we're actually sane,
we know what we can do,
without restriction.
It's just sometimes we've a problem,
between reality and fiction.
But we're not worried,
because we're near the end of the chapter,
and when we're on the outside again,
we'll drink a Guinness with rapture,
we'll put on the head phones,
and listen to some tunes,
Metallica, AC/DC,
We'll be over the moon,

So fuck you all,
we're not a rat to be tested,
we'll find a lovely lesbian,
and really molest it!

Space

Trapped on a mat determined to be kept flat,
one nights admission turns into a week,
drugs are numbing that I can hardly speak,
I'm becoming a drone with a confused depressed tone,
people keep talking, it's hard to stay in a zone.
Is it the acid or is it the meds.
On the outside I was being filled with the dreads,
I hear a voice in Dublin after visiting a church,
saying with the vision of a woman's head,
"We will fill him dread".

Spadgies

Don't try and pacify me,
apply your rues to someone else,
take a break and don't deny me,
my identity of self,
you thieves,
you rob such precious virtues,
you belittle what was son much,
respect and dignity mean nothing to you,
so I piss the Doctor off " as such ",
nod and smile,
and don't answer back,
you don't have guns to stick too,
how I'd love to hit full whack,
the rule book that you cling too,
crucify him, crucify him,
get it done and shut your mouth,
East and west believe one side,
while on the other are north and south,
'Cause conflict is your job and passion,
quarrels mean so much to you,
what pleases changes with fashions,
scoldings all there is to do,

Spanish eyes

Early morning when I wake,
within my heart,
I feel a little break,
at the realization,
that you're not there,
from the vacant space,
where your shapeless hair,
should be beside me,
on the pillow,
and your beautiful scent,
upon the air,
our limbs a tangle,
that cannot be defined,
from the beginning of yours,
to the end of mine,
the warmth of your breath,
upon my chest,
the rise and fall,
of your shapely breasts,
I wake you with a kiss,
and the feeling is bliss,
when you open your eyes,
and say I love you,
the beaming smile,

that makes everything worthwhile,
with just a hint of your cute little teeth,
I already aroused at what lies beneath,
the crumpled quilt strewn across the bed,
you slowly exhale with the turn of your head,
I tell you I love you,
you tell me the same,
a forthcoming attraction,
of when we're name and name.

Stereo

Lyrics flax the air,
exacting opinions,
from the crowd that's there,
I go pretty blank,
when I try to think of something,
but the words of songs,
make me sing,
and when I speak there's not a sound,
you could hear a penny ping,
the words that travel in my voice,
the opinions of millions,
and they've all come before me,
to dance and rejoice,
they sing and dance table tapping,
that stereo tattoo,
that was until this very day,
a by-lawed, outlawed, didgerydoo taboo.

Storm in a tea cup

When the fluid in the cup it leaves,
the tea is gone,
but there is a mystery left that weaves,
into the future,
and out of the past,
but only a discerning eye,
will know how to cast,
what was lost,
but not forgotten,
what was gained,
but left for rotten,
so appreciate with gratitude,
your hidden talent and vocation,
because it's all real life,
shot on location.

Super friend/GRASS

I trust you with my freedom,
in this game we've chosen to play,
I'm not sure who said the bullshit,
that crime it does not pay,
he wasn't as good as us,
if that's all he had to say,
life is good,
we are all sweet,
from the sugar daddy,
to the guy on the street,
but then you turned informer?
Went and got the pigs involved,
well I fucking tell you this,
I'll get you when we've revolved,
It's a long road that has no turns,
and then you'll see how it burns,
from friend to fiend,
you only get one chance,
your visas been revoked,
now you won't get a second glance.

Swell Waves

The water that day had small little ripples,
as I looked on I could feel the swell in my nipples,
so impressed by my breasts,
I decided to show the cripples,
but the wheelchair got in the way,
and with my quiff they thought I was gay,
as it turned out they were daft,
and shouted lob it in there hay!!!
So I pulled up my pants and walked away,
to mix with the passengers was my next intent,
I'll have a few snogs and make a few sprogs,
was the aim on which I was hell bent!
But sadly most of them ended up being dogs,
then before me was the angel God sent,
nothing stopped me by the end I was spent,
but she took me up wrong,
marriage was not what I meant,
but I'm still proud of my wall with that funny looking dent,
where because of the swell waves,
her head landed two foot above the vent.

The 32 Musketeers

Optical illusion,
injection or extrusion,
subliminal hit,
One slight of the hand flit,
See what you perceive,
but don't always believe,
misdirection is open,
so keep on groping,

The Bandana man

He likes his fruit,
it gives him strength,
although he may not be a superhero,
but he is to me.
He doesn't get his strength,
like banana man,
he gets it from his head band,
cos he's bandana man!
He plays his guitar,
and flies through his exams,
he finishes them in a flash.
Alacazam!
He walks out early,
with a 100%,
puts the phones in his ears,
and puts on 50 cents.
He slips on the bandana,
and now he's complete,
to do the walk and the talk,
dictated by life on the street.
Cos he's a dude,
you can tell by his clothes,
and the fuck him, fuck you attitude.

The Beautiful mind

How beautiful the mind is,
to drift along in the expanse,
gaze in the sunshine,
or a moonlit trance.
Lucid and fluid,
changing with the mood,
unlike the tides of the ocean,
a lunar attraction not yet understood.
Brightening your day,
like putting solar wind in your sails,
a quiet moment of thought almost never fails.
An up-lifting thermal from a synapse source,
of memories that are married never to divorce.
It's the only place you can get lost,
and in an instant be back,
so each time you wander,
it's safe to take the least taken track.
With its true capacity unknown,
a mystery to mankind,
never forget the power of the beautiful mind.

The day before

The excitement inside me,
is starting to build,
the void of not seeing you,
about to be filled,
before it was confirmed,
I could not let it grip,
because I know it did,
my heart it would rip,
dissapointments not strong enough,
it's a fate worse than death.

The day after

It finally happened,
I can let out my breath!!

The end

Once again,
it happens in place,
you've done it once more,
yer a fucking disgrace,
you've let yourself down,
not to mention all of us,
you're like an open wound,
seaming with puss.
A wound that won't heal,
can you sit still for a second?
And let it fucking seal.
My minds always racing,
I don't expect you to understand.
I don't or I'm not like everyone else,
fit and be normal,
be like everyone else,
please become bland,
but for me that's sinking sand,
up to the neck,
just the level that changes,
it moves in minimal ranges,
I love my family and friends,
but fuck the rest,

let them take up diving,
and get the benz.
I'll me be,
cos I love me!!!

The Galway races

To ride and run,
in the summer sun,
but it's Ireland so it's only rain.
So it's straight to the bar,
to watch from afar,
they're beautiful,
in every single way,
and that's the woman,
with their hats,
and of course the horses eating their hay,
when they run,
after their vegetarian meal,
their skirts are blown,
up around their necks,
but all that is exposed,
is their dental floss panties,
covering their lovely bums,
after 7 days running,
trying to keep on the right side of the track,
the woman are tired trying to find a rich man who is slack!
From what I hear,

there could also be horses involved,
and that they eat the slow ones at the end of the race.
If a caveman was watching,
would he just wonder how much we'd evolved?

The happy family law solicitor who's Bipolar and recovering from alchoholism

Solicit your body,
solicit your mind,
solicit your happiness,
so listen and find,
speak after thinking,
or your family will go blind,
Like the boy who cried wolf,
Bipolar or not,
if you're in the constant limelight,
you will not forget,
champagne income,
doesn't mean the same lifestyle,
because it'll all unravel,
after a while,
so head above water,
will help you recover,
and don't rule out all men,
you need at least one lover,
to start your own family,
and make some laws of your own,
and when you've done that,
you have fully grown.

The letter 'K'

First word that come to mind,
in the history of mankind,
is the second in the chain of command,
from God the father to the king,
whether or not he was willing,
this hierarchy ruled the life of every man,
and secondary to that,
is a verb quite dominant,
in every historic tale ever told,
this fruit of human's hate,
which we readily demonstrate,
"To kill" is something we have done from old,
but to kill is not bold,
if it is to break from the hold,
that Konstricts, Konditions and kontrols,
the KKK should not die,
in recent centuries,
K begins,
words with modern meanings,
as emphasis has shifted over time,
Kyoto agreement, Ku Klux Klan,
John Kerry, potentially a powerful man,
what a pity killing remains,
the commonest cime,

or swing from the poles,
and burnings to kivil and swift,
I think Kancer of the toes,
spreading up to the nose,
giving them years of tears of pain,
and we'll help them survive,
only just keeping them alive,
then let them die all over again.

The Office

Grand central to teacher Tom,
It wasn't me,
t'was the computer,
there appears to be something,
in there,
gone wrong,
I hit this,
an I hit this,
so many times,
I have the bleeps in my head,
like nursery rhymes,
well says Tom,
it's very much the same,
if you treat it all,
like playing a game,
don't approach the unit,
with utmost sheer terror,
fear no queries,
because sometimes it's not,
an operator error,
so take your time and forget,

the lords name in vein,
practice makes perfect,
and the better you'll be,
the more you train.

The Void

Oh where art thou Lloyd???
To fill my void,
you're a pain in the ass,
but your bullshit is gas,
you're the same as me,
tell them what they want,
and if it's colourful enough,
then they all can see,
but with the blinkers on,
as I've said before,
it's like breaking granite rocks,
trying to get them thinking,
outside the fucking box,
I think they'll learn,
when I begin to teach,
and if their body don't,
then their mind will reach,
so I love u baby,
I love your tools,
let's go somewhere quiet,
and push up our stools.

The Wagon

The Anti tension,
is like an AA extension,
and the dual diagnosis video,
barely merits a mention,
the alcohol and chemical,
dependence lecture,
could do with some texture,
we need recovery plan groups,
to keep us all interested,
and rally the troops,
and with perseverance,
we'll find our way,
Ni neart go cur le cheile,
Grasy the day,
sail by your own compass,
till we're finally orientated,
the need to stay on the wagon,
can't be understated!

The Wild bunch

With a bang and a crunch,
before and after lunch,
it begins as we wake,
and shape our thoughts with a rake,
run our fingers through our hair,
pretending we care,
vociferous in nature,
colossus in stature,
Assimilated and combined,
individualistically entwined,
as the day flows,
our cognitive grows,
agitated, aggravated, bolchy,
sympathetic, realistic, ballistic,
from our stratospheric head to out magma toes,
philosophy, mathematics, University of life,
we eat Geo-politics,
without even a scrunch of strife,
so try your tactics,
because to us it's tic-tacs,
you may think you're smart,
but this is only the start,
we haven't even begun,
on a count of three,

we haven't even reach one,
conquer after divide,
you better run and hide,
we see your intentions,
before your thoughts collide,
solidarity is key,
but nature finds a way,
we may piss you off,
but our future's ours together,
into the foray.

Throw Away Our Note

You've the right to a yes,
You've a right to a no,
You've the right to ponder,
Or go with the flow,
So get of the fence,
and stop spouting cents,
that's designed to intrigue,
by causing fatigue,
firing imaginations with great wealth and gold,
and how everything beneath heaven can always be sold,
it's a sellers market,
we're always being told,
so let's give them a creation,
that's 3 in 1 bold.
We'll fire their brains from great distance and length,
an up-heavel so taciturn that their
reticence will lose stength,
we'll dangle the angle and show them the square of the hair,
and as the cube of the tube goes scoobadoobdoob,
we'll dance our jig on our universal Rubix lube.
We're slippy and sliddy and all out good fun,
but always remember one thing about us,
We'll never turn and run!

Together

If like they say,
what's for you,
won't go by you,
then there's no need for me to feel blue,
I think of you when we are apart,
even though our journey's just beginning,
we haven't even passed start!
I follow my heart,
but I have faith in my mind,
God must be missing an angel,
maybe he sent you to me,
as a gift of a kind,
I enjoy the talk,
and when we walk the walk,
I like your confidence,
and sure footed approach,
your feelings for me,
no-one could reproach,
so follow your heart,
and lead with your mind,
and tell all the doubters,
you've met one of a KIND!!!

Tree-leave

Does a leave leave a tree,
or a tree leave a leave,
they're parting company together,
from tree to leave and you're tree to leave,
where the wind blows,
will keep you on your toes,
from noon day sun,
to frigid night has begun,
so go young one,
find your own shelter,
may your life be like everyones,
Helter Skelter!!!

Trinity college?

So you want to go there?
Why ever for?
Well my friend from sea is here,
studying Maths and French,
and he said I might find,
myself a good wench.
She'll be smart, she'll be funny,
whatever about her looks,
but talent for thought provoke,
you won't rebuke,
it's a great atmosphere,
to immerse yourself in,
and if you want the best out of life,
then this is where to begin,
no matter what you study,
from keyhole surgery to knitting,
they'll fill your brain,
till the sides are splitting,
so I took on-board what he said,
and thought to myself,
while lying in bed,
that's me, sign up,

where do I pay?
Carpe diem,
Grasp the day!
I wrote this to get out.

Truth

Well doctor Slim,
it's been a blast,
I've made a lot of new friends,
and they're not in the past,
between the patients and the staff,
we've had a laugh,
at first I didn't understand,
the blatant reticence,
and your reluctance to move me,
but now it makes sense,
the drugs do work,
not like the song said,
and the lack of activity,
made room in my bed,
I've slept the sleep,
of a thousand dreams,
yet I did not die,
or wake up with screams,
so I take back what I said,
both to your face,
and behind your back,
it wasn't all that bad,
just that your visiting was slack!

But you're busy people,
and this I comprehend,
and I now firmly believe,
you've all been a God send!

Turbulence

The early worm,
catches the flight,
destination unknown,
what's the movie,
on the menu tonight?
then it feels the crunch,
and begins to squirm,
the feeling of dread,
travels from tail to head,
high it glides,
through the early morning light,
the landing pad of the nest,
is now in sight,
the hungriest of the chicks,
is always fed last,
the loudest of them all,
stands proud and tall,
pushes the rest aside,
who are left to fast,
but the others learn a lesson,
of how to survive.

Unito

Into the outside,
outside to the in,
it's inside out,
when the outsides in.
Where to begin?
Oh where to get in??
Begin at the start,
when starting a beginning,
first impressions last,
so you need a formula 4 winning,
talk in their subject,
talk in their tongue,
explain to everyone,
that their foot is on the rung,
and that there is one definite thing,
that is defo in life,
no matter how your hat is hung,
no matter what they say or tell,
you're the air that feeds this lung.

14th of August 2003

University of life

So now I start from the beginning of the page,
no hands of anger or inner rage,
not a childs delight to see a fight,
if even only,
the words of jest,
if they do it once,
then they do it lest,
as for now and in the future,
the cage of rage is closed wide shut,
but it was all a stage,
and boy could we perform.
My best education for how to be norm.
I THANK MY PARENTS for what I've got,
and not jealous for what I have not,
if or is GODS will or not -
I read a bit a bible and oh my god,
I nearly become a disciple.
I took a double take -
What's that you say GOD?
Don't make a mistake?
I believe this true but what am I to do -
I look and walk and talk like you?
We run Gods course of a little remorse,
and when we look guilt free enough,

You're are outta the rough,
rolling away on the lovely fairway.
So mistake I think not,
But that's not our lot.
So take it as it comes -
you may not like it but acceptance will
make you feel like you had it.
Begrudge no man who has made his
money by his own hand,
for he is the man who can carry the
world upon his shoulders,
and laugh and luck at life through the eyes of a child,
he will be the man who puts the letters 'l'i'm'd' in mild.
So to continue the tail,
when in circles for a minute.
The University of life taught by
daddy,mammy,sisiter,bro and the ducklings.

Reason:

Just admitted....nothing!!!!!!!!!

Verse

Drink when you're happy,
Drink when you're sad,
Drink when you're happy,
Drink when you're lonely,
Drink when you're mad,
Drink when you're worried,
Drink when you're scared,
Drink to feel good,
Drink to feel better,
Drinking the beer,
slowly opening the letter,
good news or bad?
Will he or won't he?
Don't mind him,
he's jack the lad,
loves to be loved,
centre of it all,
running out of chances,
breaking down the wall,
the wall is unstable,
cracks starting to show,
so much to lose,
learning to slow,
not as smart,

so much to learn,
of older and wiser,
keep an eye on my stern,
only one answer,
answer is plain,
learn to control,
if not then abstain,
can't control,
when mind in a frame,
think of it now,
causes pain,
light in the tunnel,
oncoming train?
Keep mind focused,
strong on the goal,
think of my girl,
look into the soul,
are you the man,
or are you a mouse?
Go to it,
and do it,
think of your house,

stand up and be counted,
must look after her soul,
guard with your life,
and you'll end up in pole.

W.A.B.C

I'm sitting on the toilet sun,
thinking how the day begun,
a decade of life has passed us by,
but there's so much out there left to try,
enough to stop the boredom and cry,
situations to get out of intact,
let's go to the station in the caravan and distract,
and foul is fair and fair is foul,
we'll raise a shit storm,
with our 0.22 trowel,
first you tell us,
we can write our names,
and true to form we begin our games,
till all that is left is a pissed off DJ,
and big black letter's saying CON & JAMES,
throw us out?
Annoy at your pearl,
but you've done it now,
so there's no going back,
our little hatched plan of destruction,
was just put firmly on track,
with misdirection,
we acquired the gun,
but who's gonna point it?

as we fought one on one,
so jamsie pshyced the hell out of me,
telling me I've got a brilliant kick,
stealth fully through the first open door,
slick listening out for the talking tard,
I blasted the studio open,
Jamesie shouted "freeze ya bastard!",
Happy with a job well done,
as he fell apart at the sight of the gun,
there's the bigman shitless,
wonder now,
mooin over the airwaves like a cow,
misdirection puts the gun back in place,
then off to some mischief we race,
till the day we die,
we never forget his face,
we'll have plenty of more stories to tell,
but it's really like a bottomless well,
so that was one of the stories of fun,
but they aren't over yet,
not by a million billion barrels and then some!!

War and Peace

Churchill said,
"War is only just,
when all other means of peace is exhausted"
So pick your political target,
and shoot it or blast it.
Not like the Americans,
who use collateral damage,
by bombing schools and hospitals,
creating colossal carnage.
What's their agenda?
Is it war and peace?
Or a piece of war?
They enjoy the power rush,
like driving a fast car,
overwhelmed and inebriated,
by the exuberance of their own verbosity.
They plunder and pillage,
all non-American cities,
countries a far from their own lovely land,
and the only disasters they receive,
is by the act of Gods hand,
two buildings are flattened,
to ground zero,
and the fucking yanks,

think George Dubwa a hero?
Let's see what they say think,
when his true intentions are shown,
When his thoughts of world domination,
are fully grown.
But the Irish won't let him,
we'll stand tall and be counted,
no prouder a nation there is on this earth,
we'll smile at the grandiose delusions.
But we'll hide our mirth,
I don't believe in war,
because I don't like fighting,
but we're warriors at heart,
It comes natural to us,
so we'll hit the same spot,
twice with a single bolt of lightning!
So come on Mr. Presidente,
bring it on,
because you ain't never met anyone like me,
My name is CON!

Weekender Bender

The ultimate cyclone,
that's bored us to the bone,
a tough day doing nothing,
3 days rolled into one,
we've had our visitors,
but they've come and gone,
all work stops friday,
if you work 9 to 5,
little thought of us,
some distraction to keep us alive,
we're afraid to get to happy,
for fear they'll think we're high,
but we all play our games,
and always on the sly,
and at night when were pacing,
that worn path of a corridor,
that the many have them facing,
a weekends a week long,
but drug us enough and we mightn't notice,
sure they'll talk to each other,
and enlighten each other like the leaf of the lotus,
the best help we get in here,

is the help from each other,
we only need the walls,
to hold the roof,
and we turn a blind eye to those who are aloof.

What lies within

The kiss,
the gift,
the smile,
the yawn,
like the first rays of light,
just at the dawn,
the sense of beginning,
the start of something new,
the turning of blackness into blue,
like the spiritual feeling,
after a well said mass,
or the cool smell of freshness,
from a summer evenings cut grass,
dormant emotions beneath my skin,
you brought them out from deep within,
heightened awareness of the beauty around me,
like so many who look,
but do not see,
beneath your beauty,
which is so pleasing to the eyes,
lies so much more hidden in disguise,
I've discovered some,
and I want to see more,

you'll never get rid of me,
now you've opened up the door,
I feel your strength,

and see your resolve,
and I'm honoured there's a part,
for me to involve,
In your life and in your future,
in which you'll never tire,
because burning inside you,
is the eternal fire.

Who, me, I...?

So you think you know me?
Or so you say,
to underestimate me,
would be a regrettable day,
not for me,
but most definitely you,
a condescending attitude,
that would make some people sue,
So you know my mind?
Even sussed out my thinking,
realized with ease,
why I was always drinking,
taking some herbs,
medicinal dope,
yet I confuse the hell out of ye,
when I say God bless the Pope,
you see your problem is,
now I'm not telling you your job,
ye've got ears but don't listen,
that's your prob,
if we use 10% of our brain,
that leaves 90 uncharted,
yet you say you know me,
don't get me started,

if you don't know yourself,
how can you know me?
I see doubt in your eyes,
it's like you're lost @ sea,
up shit creak in a barbed wire canoe,
oh no we've sprung a leak,
what can we do?
Bucketless, paddleless, look at the hole,
the secrets to my life,
are under lock and key in my soul.

Windows

Lined with lashes,
and glistening brightly,
taking in daylight,
and taking rest nightly,
beauty and depth,
windows to the soul,
meaning and life,
even when old,

reflected in them,
is the sight that they see,
and on the horizon,
all speckled with trees,
a vision of beauty,
just life as it looks,
the dust of earth,
to the flight of the rooks.

Deserts so far stretching,
quite different from here,
no deserts out windows,
where falsehood is cheer,
windows are smudged,
with the dust of the day,

down slides the tear,
as I look to the grey,

.

a view of the monotony,
so unlike the ideal,
the distance of desert,
not near what is real,
but windows provide,
an alternative world,
much opportunity,
soon to be unfurled.

Windows

Framed at every corner,
no matter where you turn,
for all the right reasons,
I'm forever less than taciturn.
Your field of vision always stable,
whatever happens within the view,
from the changing of the seasons,
to life's characters that you construe.
Moving closer to the pane,
the lifeguard of your soul,
it's who you are,
not what you do,
beyond your reason and control.
Peripherals now inspected,
what's there was there before,
it's just you didn't see it,
while standing at the door.
If you look to see close up,
eyes open taking in,
you learn to see while standing back,
the different sounds within the din.

Occidental, oriental,north and south,
each have all the traits,
it's the nature of the lookers,
that decide on all their fates.

Words of scrabble

Sitting right here now in the morning still,
listening to the birds and their first light shrill,
the drone of the traffic drundling by,
the reason behind the question,
becomes less and less why?
But more of an answer the more I learn,
and the worries of people,
becomes less of a concern.
They're starting to believe,
as long as I don't go to fast,
and someday very soon,
the knowledge we impart will stay fixed and last.

Reasons:
This was written later on that morning
after writing Bedtime.

You are all @ sea

On the end of the phone,
is the end of that line,
but it's the start of another,
a magnificent maze for a mine,
dig out the truth,
from underneath your feet,
the soil is soft,
waiting to meet and greet,
to answer your question,
of the struggling fleet,
so with a lick of paint,
to make the accountants faint,
cos a half measure man I ain't,
sunrise to sunset,
the fleet'll sail proud,
and from over their eyes,
remove the shrouds.